"I need protection and I am willing to pay for it," Violet said.

His fingers turned and curled over hers, eyes rising to lock into her own.

"How?"

"I can see that you want me. You would not have come here otherwise."

He laughed at that. "You are bold, Violet Addington, but are you also foolish?"

"I am a twenty-seven-year-old widow who is soon to be twenty-eight. It is not permanence I am petitioning you for, only safety. I have not offered my body to any other and there have been many who have asked." She couldn't make it any plainer.

Author Note

Aurelian de la Tomber, Comte de Beaumont, was one of the main lesser characters in my last book, *A Night of Secret Surrender*.

He fascinated me not only with his cleverness and his danger but also because of his vulnerability. I wanted to know more of his story and his life. I felt that his utter darkness needed the counterpoint of a woman who brought him the light.

Lady Violet Addington has suffered her own losses, too, but she is a woman of resilience and purpose.

Can the secrets that lie between them bridge the gap of politics, greed and history?

Can love overcome darkness?

SOPHIA JAMES

*A Proposition
for the Comte*

Recycling programs
for this product may
not exist in your area.

ISBN-13: 978-1-335-05181-3

A Proposition for the Comte

Copyright © 2018 by Sophia James

Sophia James lives in Chelsea Bay, on the North Shore of Auckland, New Zealand, with her husband, who is an artist. She has a degree in English and history from Auckland University and believes her love of writing was formed by reading Georgette Heyer on vacations at her grandmother's house. Sophia enjoys getting feedback at sophiajames.co.

Books by Sophia James

Harlequin Historical

Ruined by the Reckless Viscount

Gentlemen of Honor

A Night of Secret Surrender
A Proposition for the Comte

The Society of Wicked Gentlemen

A Secret Consequence for the Viscount

The Penniless Lords

Marriage Made in Money
Marriage Made in Shame
Marriage Made in Rebellion
Marriage Made in Hope
Once Upon a Regency Christmas
"Marriage Made at Christmas"

Visit the Author Profile page
at Harlequin.com for more titles.

Chapter One

London 1815

Aurelian de la Tomber felt the bullet rip through his arm, rebounding off bone and travelling on to some further softer place in his side. Standing perfectly still, he waited, for life, or for death, his blood racing as vision lightened.

After a long moment he wondered if he might lose consciousness altogether and be found here by others in this damning position, caught red-handed and without excuse. Catching his balance, he breathed in hard and fast, his mind calculating all the variables in the situation as he struggled for logic.

The bullet had patently not pierced an artery for the flow from his wounds was already slowing. The heavy beat of blood in his ears suggested that his heart still worked despite the intrusion and, with careful movement, his impaired balance might also be manageable. That he could even reason any of this out was another plus and if the sweat on his forehead and upper lip was building he knew this to be a normal part of shock. Still, he had no idea of how deep the bullet had gone and the pain numbed in the first moment of impact was rising. A good sign that, he thought, for in the quickening of discomfort lay the first defence in a body's quest for living.

The man before him was dead and no longer any threat, the blood from his neck pooling on to a thick rug. Kicking away the gun, Aurelian turned to the door. People would have heard the shot, he was certain of it, for the upmarket boarding house on Brompton Place was well inhabited. Unlacing his neckcloth, he used his teeth to anchor the end of the fabric before winding it as tightly as he could around his upper arm. It was all he could do for now. It would staunch the flow and allow him a passage of escape. Hopefully.

When he began to shake he cursed, the world blurring before him and moving in a strange and convoluted way. It felt as if he was on the deck of a ship in a storm, his footfalls not quite where he placed them, the roiling world making him nauseous.

'*Merde.*'

The expletive was short and harsh. He had to get as far from here as he could before he collapsed. Placing his good hand against the wall, he counted the rises. Fourteen on one set of stairs and another fourteen on the next. He always knew how many steps went up or down in every building he entered, for it was part of his training and laxity led to mistakes. His breathing was laboured and he coughed to hide the noise as he passed by the small blue room to one side of the lobby. He was relieved to see that the watcher who'd been there when he arrived a quarter of an hour ago was now absent.

The front door was ten footfalls from the base of the stairs, the fourth tile risen and badly cracked, then the door handle was in his grasp. Blood made his fingers slip from the metal and he wiped his palm against his jacket before trying again.

Finally he was out, the cold of the night on his face, a blustery nor'wester, he reasoned as he turned, the stone wall a new anchor, a way to walk straight. His nails dug into the crumbling mortar, scraggly plants reaching up from the pathway and smelling of something akin to the chestnuts roasting on open fires on the Champs-Élysées at Christmas.

That wasn't right, he thought.

There were no vendors at this time of night in Brompton Place in Chelsea. He closed his eyes and then opened them again quickly. Brompton Road lay before him and then Hyde Park. If he could get there he would be safe, for the greenery would hide him. He could take stock of things in solitude and stuff his jacket with grass to staunch the blood. If he followed the tree lines he could find sanctuary and silence. It was cold and the fingers on his left hand felt strange, the pins and needles lessening now down to nothingness.

If this had been Paris, he thought, he would have known countless alleys to simply disappear into and numerous contacts from whom to find help. He swore again, only this time his voice sounded distant and hollow.

Falling heavily, he knew he could no longer stand, but there was a grate that led to an underground drain in the gutter and he crawled there until his fingers closed on cold metal. He lifted the covering, straining for all he was worth, the weight of the thing throwing him backwards on to the road, slick with the black ice of a freezing January morning. His head took the knock of it as he slammed against the cobbles.

The sound of carriage wheels close by was his last thought before a tunnel of darkness took him in.

Violet Augusta Juliet, the Dowager Viscountess Addington, should never have encouraged the Honourable Alfred Bigglesworth to air his opinions on horseflesh because all night she had been forced to pay attention to them. No, she should have smiled nicely and moved on when he first waylaid her at the Barringtons' ball, but there had been something in his expression that looked rather desperate and so she had listened.

It was both her best and worst point, she thought, this worry for other people's feelings and her need to make them…happy. She shook her head and turned to gaze out of the carriage window and into the darkness. *Happy* was not quite the word she sought. *Valued* was a better one, perhaps. Frowning at such ruminations, she removed her gloves. She'd never liked her hands wrapped in fabric and it was a nightly habit of hers to tear off the strictures as soon as she was able. Her cap followed.

'Mr Bigglesworth seemed to have taken your fancy, Violet?'

Amaryllis Hamilton sat beside her in the carriage, dark eyes observant, and Violet felt a spurt of guilt for she'd meant to leave earlier as she knew her sister-in-law had only recently recovered from a malady of the chest.

She continued, 'He is said to be a sterling catch and those who know him speak highly of the family.'

Her tone was playful and dimples showed plainly, but Violet hoped Amara might have said all she wanted to. However, she was not yet finished.

'You deserve a good man to walk in life beside you, Violet, and I pray nightly to the Lord above that you might yet find one.'

This was a conversation that had been ongoing across the past twelve months between them, but to-night Violet was irritated by it. 'I have attained the grand old age of twenty-seven, Amara, and I am not on the lookout for another husband. Thank goodness.'

That echo of honesty had her sitting up straighter, the wedding ring on her left hand catching at the light.

She remembered when Harland had placed it on her finger under a window of stained glass and beside a vase filled with lilies.

She'd never liked the flowers since, the sheen on waxy petals somehow synonymous with the sweat across her new husband's brow. Avaricious. Relieved. A coupling written in law and not easily broken. Her substantial dowry in his hands and her father stand-ing there with a broad smile upon his face.

The carriage had now slowed to pass through the narrow lanes off Brompton Road and then it stopped altogether—which was unusual given that the traffic at this time of the early morning should have been negligible.

Pushing back the curtain, Violet peered out and saw a man lying there. A gentleman, by the style of his clothing, though he was without his necktie and was more than rumpled looking. Unlatching the window, she called out to her driver.

'Is there some problem, Reidy?'

'It's nothing, my lady. Just a drunk who's fallen asleep on the throughway. The young footman is trying to remove him to a safer distance as we speak. We shall be off again in a moment.'

Violet glanced down and saw the half-truth of such a statement, for the Addington footman was a slight lad who was having a good deal of trouble in dragging the larger man to safety. The glint of dark blood caught what little light there was and without hesitation she opened the door and slipped out of the carriage.

'He is hurt and will need to be seen by a doctor straight away.' A heavy gash in the hairline above his right ear had spread blood across his face and there was a bandage wrapped about the top half of his left arm. His eyes opened at the sound of her voice, but she had no true picture of his visage in the midnight gloom.

'I…will…be…fine.' It was almost whispered, irritated and impatient.

She bent down. 'Fine to lie here and die from loss

of blood, sir, or fine to simply freeze in the cold of this night?'

Her driver had brought forth a light and the stranger's smile heartened her. If he was indeed dying, she did not imagine he would find humour in anything. Laying one hand across his own, she felt it to be frozen.

'Bring him into the carriage. Owing to the lateness of the hour and the falling temperature, I think it wise to deliver him home ourselves without further ado.'

With a struggle the servants righted him and Violet saw that he was tall, towering a good way above her own five foot six.

He swore in fluent French, too, a fact that made her stiffen and take in breath. Then he was sick all over his boots, the look of horror on his face plain.

'Find the water bottle and sluice him down.'

Her driver's frown was heavy. 'It seems the man might be better left to go his own way, my lady.'

'Please do as I say, Reidy. It is cold out here and I should like to be inside the warmth of the carriage.'

'Yes, ma'am.'

The water soaked her own silken slippers as it tumbled from the man's Hessians on to the icy street. As the stranger wiped the blood from around his mouth with the fabric of his sleeve, a scar across the lower part of his chin was much more easily detected.

He looked like a pirate dragged in from battle, dangerous, huge and unknown, his dark hair loose and his eyes caught in the half-light to gleam a furious and glittering gold.

'Where do you live, sir?' She asked this question

as soon as she had him settled, instructing her driver to wait and see which direction he required.

But even as he coughed and tried to speak his eyes simply rolled back and he toppled against the cushioned leather.

'We will make for home. He needs warmth and a physician.'

'You are certain, my lady?'

'I am. Mrs Hamilton will see that I am unharmed and the young footman can join us inside. If there is any difficulty at all we will bang loudly on the roof. In his state, I hardly think that he constitutes a threat.'

As the conveyance began to move, Violet looked across at the new arrival. She thought he was awkwardly placed, the stranger, his good arm caught in an angle beneath him. He held a weapon in his pocket and another in the soft leather of his right boot. She could see the swell of the haft of a blade.

Armed and unsafe. She should throw him out right now on to the street where another might find him. Yet she did not.

He was wounded and the strange vulnerability of a strong man bent into unconsciousness played at her heartstrings.

It had begun to sleet, too, the weather sealing them into a small and warm cocoon as they wound their way back to her town house. Soon it would snow hard for the storm clouds across the city last evening had been purple. Further off towards the river, bands of freezing rain blurred the horizon. She shivered and then ground her teeth, top against bottom with the thought of all that she had done.

Impetuous. Foolish. How often had Harland said that of her? A woman of small and insignificant opinion. A woman who never quite got things right. Amara was observing her with uncertainty and even the footman had trouble meeting her eyes. The price of folly, she thought, yet if she had left him he would have died, she was certain of it.

Arriving home, she bade her servants to help the driver to carry the man in and sent a footman off to fetch the physician.

'At this time of night he may be difficult to find, my lady.'

'All I ask is that you hurry, Adams, and instruct the doctor that he shall be paid well when he comes.'

Placing her guest in a bedchamber a good few doors down from her own, Violet ignored Amara's qualms.

'He does not look like a tame man,' her sister-in-law offered, watching from the doorway. 'He does not quite look English, either.'

She was right. He looked nothing like the milk-sop lords they had waded through tonight at the Barringtons' ball. His dress was too plain and his hair was far longer than any man in the *ton* would have worn theirs. He looked menacing and severe and beautiful. Society would tiptoe around a man like this, not quite knowing how to categorise him. Left in a bedchamber filled with ruffled yellow fabric and ornate fragile furniture he was badly misplaced. His natural home looked to be far more rudimentary than this.

'Clean him up, Mrs Kennings, and find him one of my late husband's nightshirts. The doctor should be here in a short while. Choose others to help you.'

The clock struck the half-hour as she walked past the main staircase to the library. She no longer felt tired. She felt alive and somewhat confused as to her reaction to this whole conundrum.

Harland had insisted that every decision had been his to make and she had seldom had a hand in it. Tonight there was a sort of freedom dancing in the air, a possibility of all that could be, another layer between who she had been and who she was to become.

If the servants wondered at her orders they didn't say, obeying her and refraining from further query. Power held a quiet energy that was gratifying.

A knock on the door of her library a few moments later brought a footman inside the room with an armful of weapons. 'Mrs Kennings sent me in with these, my lady. She said she thought they were better off here than on the stranger's person. The doctor has just arrived, too.'

'Ask him to come and see me when he has finished then, Adams. I shall wait for him in here.'

'Very well.'

She noted the armaments were many and varied as she looked over the array on the table. A flintlock pistol made of walnut and steel sat before her, the brass butt plate catching the light. A well-weighted piece, she thought, as she lifted it and wondered at its history. A selection of knives sat to one side: a blade wedged into rough leather; a longer, sharper knife with a handle of inlaid shell; and a thicker, broader half-sword, the haft engraved with some ancient design.

The tools of his trade and a violent declaration of intent. Such a truth was as undeniable as it was shocking. This man she had helped was a dealer in death, a pillager of lives. She wondered how being such would have marked him. Perhaps at this very moment Mrs Kennings was lifting away the fabric of his shirt to show the doctor the scars written on his skin as a history.

She was sure it would be so. A darkness of blood was smeared across the dull grey of the sword's steel where it had bitten into bone and flesh only recently. She imagined what the other opponent might now look like and crossed to the cabinet to pour herself a brandy.

She had not drunk anything stronger than a spiced punch in all the years of her marriage. Now she found herself inclined to brandy for the spirit took away some of her pain, though she was always careful to drink alone. The brandy slid down her throat like a warm tonic, settling in her stomach and quelling her nerves.

She wanted to rise and go to the stranger just to make certain that he was not dead. She wanted to touch him again, too, and feel the heat of his skin, to know that he breathed. Tilting her head, she listened for any sign of footsteps, glad when they did not come, for if the moments multiplied it could only mean he lived.

The dead would not hold a physician here for an extended length of time and a medic expecting payment would be quick to come to the library and claim what was owed.

She heard a deep cry of pain and tensed, the ensuing silence just as potent as the noise had been. She imagined the treatment that he was now being subjected to as the doctor tried to make sense of his wounds.

'Please, God, help him.' She whispered these words into the night and looked across at the fire burning in the grate.

The maid must have been roused from the warmth of her bed to set it. Sometimes the unfairness in life was a never-ending carousel—a misfortune here, a death there, the nuisance of it left as a past-midnight duty for those who served their masters even in exhaustion.

Harland was a part of it, too, with his immorality and anger. After their first few months together she had rarely seen him happy. She frowned. The events of the evening were making her maudlin and there was no point in looking back on all that had been so shattering.

Her father's words were in the mix there, too. When he had seen her off into the arms of Harland Addington, he had leaned down and given his advice.

'The Viscount is a man going places, a clever and titled young man. He will do you well, Violet, you will see.'

She had imagined at the time he'd believed it, but

now she was not so certain. Her father had been a hard
and distant parent whose personal relationships had
faltered consistently.

They had hated each other after a few years together, her stepmother and father, almost with the
same heated distaste that she and Harland had regarded one another by the end of it all. Like father like
daughter. Lost in the tricky mire of right and wrong.

A noise in the passageway twenty-five minutes later
had her turning and she put the empty second glass of
brandy on the table and waited for the door to open.

'Dr Barry is ready to depart, my lady.' Her housekeeper stood at the old physician's side. Violet vaguely
recognised the man. Perhaps Harland had had him
here at the town house before to diagnose one of his
many and varied physical complaints.

'How does the patient fare?'

'Poorly, I am afraid, Lady Addington.' She knew
from the expression on his face that the prognosis
was not a hopeful one. 'The whole site is swollen. If
God in all his wisdom wants him to recover then he
might, but if not…'

He left the sentiment hanging for a second before he
carried on. 'A man of violence must take his chances
with the angels or the demons.'

'Are there instructions for his care?'

'There are, my lady. Make certain he takes in water
and apply this salve to his right temple and left arm
every six hours. I have a compress in place at his side
under the bandage and will change that in the morn-

ing. The ribcage is the area of the most worry, but the bullet has been removed. I will return on the morrow at the noon hour to examine him again unless you would wish to have him taken from here…'

'No, I do not.' She barely knew where that reply came from and the doctor looked surprised.

'Very well, Lady Addington. I have left my receipt and wish you well for what remains of this night. If he dies by the morning, send word. I'll come for the body.'

Nodding, she swallowed away any thank you she had been about to offer. Violet had expected more grace, honour and hope in one whose path in life was to tend to the needs of the sick. She would not let him call again, she swore it.

Moments later she was perched on a chair by her tall stranger's bed, the weight of her decision to bring him into her custody firming upon her shoulders.

He was even more beautiful without the blood and the dirt. She could see that in the first second of observing him. Better for him to have been plain and homely, for Harland had been as remarkably handsome and look at what had happened there.

Shaking her head, she concentrated on the man before her, glad to be alone with him, glad for the night-time and the candles and the half-forgotten world outside.

Her housekeeper had dressed him in one of Harland's starched and embroidered gowns, the collar of it stiff about his neck. The gash above his ear had been stitched and his long dark hair fell over the yellow ointment smeared across the wound. Nothing could hide the mark on his chin, though, a scar just under the side of his mouth and curling beneath his neck. A knife wound, Violet thought, that had been left untended till it festered for it was no cleanly healed injury at all. She wondered at the pain of such a wound.

He was hot. She could see this in the bloom of his skin and the stretched closeness of bone, the pulse in his throat skittering and thready.

'Let him live,' she pleaded to no one in particular, though she supposed it was to God that she made this entreaty. It had been a long time since she had prayed with any sincerity.

He was pale and the dark bruising of tiredness lay beneath closed eyes. His nails were short and well trimmed, the ring he wore brought into full relief by the light in the room. It was crested and fashioned out of a heavy gold, a row of small diamonds caught under an engraved coronet.

He had lost the top of the third finger on his right hand, a clean healed cut that spoke of intent and expertise, but a relatively old wound for the scarring was opaque and faded. A man with life drawn upon him like a story and tonight with more chapters adding to the tale. The bed barely contained his height, his knees bent so that his feet did not overlap the base board. The boots placed beside the bed were of the finest leather, the buckles heavy, well fashioned and expensive, the same coronet of the ring engraved in silver.

With a sigh she stood and turned to the window,

looking out across the city and the tableau of fading lights. London felt safe and busy. It felt peopled and close with the movement and the noise and the constant change of things to see. She had been here for twelve months now and had not once left the central district of the town. An ordered life with nothing surprising in it. Why had she then insisted that this dangerous golden-eyed stranger be brought home?

Taking up the book she had brought in with her, she sat again on the chair by the bed and began to read aloud. She'd heard somewhere that connections to the living world were advantageous to those knocking on the door of the next one, for it brought them back, guiding them.

Half an hour later when he spoke she almost jumped.

'Where…am…I?' His tongue wet the dryness of his lips, each word carefully enunciated.

'In Chelsea at my town house. I am Violet, Lady Addington, sir, and we found you wounded on Brompton Place in the very early hours of this morning. When you were unable to give us your address we brought you here.'

'We?' The one word held a wealth of questions.

The quiet blush of blood ran across her cheeks. It was the curse of having such a fair skin and she gritted her teeth in fury. She had no need to explain any of her circumstances to him and she would not. Ignoring his query, she went on.

'You have a substantial wound in the hairline above

your right ear. It has bled profusely, though it has now been stitched. You also have a bullet hole in your left side which travelled through your arm to enter your ribcage. It has been removed, but the doctor who was summoned to tend to you is not certain of the effects it might engender. My housekeeper, however, insists she has seen others with your malady up and walking within a matter of days.'

In point of fact, Mrs Kennings had said a lot more than that about the patient, Violet thought, but was not about to repeat her servant's fervent appreciation of the more favourable parts of his body.

'Did anyone follow me here?'

The horror of such a question had her staring. 'No. Did you expect them to?'

He turned his head away.

'Where are my clothes?'

'They were filthy, sir. We placed a nightgown upon you and tucked you into bed. There are garments you can wear in the drawer across the room when you recover. Your own clothes shall be returned to you on the morrow.'

'And my weapons?'

'Are being cleaned. I think you need to rest, for it was the opinion of my driver that you would feel dizzy if you moved too fast.'

'He was right.'

He raised his hand against the light to shade his eyes. A headache, perhaps?

'I do not think it was a robber who hurt you.'

'No. I do not think that, either.'

His diction was aristocratic and old-fashioned. He spoke as if every word needed to be carefully said and thought about. She had the vague impression that perhaps English was not his first language and another worry surfaced as she remembered how he had sworn in French when first she had found him.

'Who exactly are you, sir?'

This time Violet allowed more sharpness into her tone.

The woman peering at him was beautiful. He hadn't seen such colouring on anyone before, with her green-grey eyes, stark white skin and hair that fell around a finely sculpted face in a blaze of red glory. She also looked uncertain, her full lips parted and the tip-tilt of her nose above giving her the appearance of an angel newly delivered from Heaven. A sun-kissed one at that, given her freckles.

Shaking his head hard, he imagined her as an illusion resulting from the blow to his temple and the shot in his side, but when he looked again all the parts of Violet Addington were still assembled in such a startling comeliness.

Violet. She suited her name. Delicate. Unadorned. Fragile. A hint of steel was there, too, as well as a baffling openness.

Lady Addington? Why would she be in a bedchamber with him across the depths of a frigid London night wearing a dark green high-necked ballgown with her hair down?

Nothing quite made sense.

'Why are you here with me alone?' He did not wish to give her his name for it meant some involvement in his life that she could not help but be hurt by. He was pleased when he saw her measure the truth of his reticence and look away. If he could have dragged himself off the bed and got to the door there and then, he would have, but nothing seemed to be working properly and he was so damnably tired.

'You were reading me a story about the Spartans?'

She smiled. 'I imagined you might enjoy it. You look a little like one of those ancient warriors yourself.'

'In an embroidered nightshirt?'

'Oh, it's not your clothes I am speaking of, but your disposition. One would need to be more than dangerous to be allowed within their ranks. It's a certain peril, an expectation, a darkness that does not allow in the light.'

'Well, you're right about that at least.'

Shadows crossed her face, a frown marking a line on her forehead. 'I should probably leave you to sleep.'

He closed his eyes momentarily as he nodded and when he opened them again she was gone.

She barely slumbered that night, but lay tense and fidgety in her bed, listening for any sound of movement, but hearing none at all from his chamber at the end of the corridor. Was he asleep or did he lie there as she did, eyes wide open with expectation?

He had not wanted to give her his name which meant there were secrets he wished hidden. His weapons were back at his side now and she wondered if that was a safe thing to have done for the well-being of her household. But his query as to whether anyone had followed them also rang loud in her head.

Did he expect more trouble? Was he a man whom others could be hunting even at this moment along the wealthy streets of Chelsea and Knightsbridge? If peril were indeed to arrive at her door would he be able to protect them all? Or was *he* the peril?

The clock in her room beat out the hour of four and still she felt sleep far away. Once she had seldom slept at all through the night, day after day of restless slumber ending only when her husband's factor had come up from the stables with a solemn face to pronounce Harland dead from an accident.

Nowadays she slept a little better, if not dreamlessly, the city enveloping her with its noise and its toil; the sort of rest that had taken the circles from beneath her eyes. The dragging lethargy was gone, but often she felt the self-blame of doubt.

Could she ever regain the girl she had once been before her marriage, the one who had thought the world open and good and fair? The one who was not so scared of life?

She turned her wedding ring on her finger, wishing she could simply tear it off and be done with memories, but there were expectations here in society and requirements for grief, even if the emotion did not exist in her. She could not expunge the memory of Harland completely from either her person or from the town house without such vehemence tossing up questions. Questions she could ill afford to answer.

She felt old and dried up, today's unexpected ending so out of the ordinary that she was certain it would all finish badly, just as everything else in her life so far had.

The stranger had been hurt many times, the doctor had said and so had her housekeeper, for his skin was marked with years of violence. The stillness in him magnified his danger, too, his observation menacing. He gave an impression that he was just waiting for his time to strike, marking out his territory, lying there injured and pale but with watchfulness alive in his eyes.

It was as if she had invited a Bengal tiger to sit down with her for supper. She could already feel the damage he might leave for he was far from tame, perhaps temporarily muzzled and bridled by his substantial injuries, but undeniably perilous. She would be a fool to think otherwise.

The anger in her rose and sleep seemed a long way off.

She woke up with a start, her heart pounding, and the clock at her bedside pointing to the late hour of ten. Was he dead? Had the doctor come again? Was the world changed in a way that might make everything different? Why had no one woken her? All these questions went around and around as she sat and rang the small silver bell to summon her maid.

Edith came with her usual bustle, though this morning she had news to impart. 'When Mrs Kennings went in early to check on the newcomer the bed was made and the gown was folded. The junior maid said he was not in bed when she came to stoke the fires just after six, my lady. She said that he was a neat and tidy guest, though, and that he left you a note. I put it in my pocket here to give to you the moment you woke so that it would not be lost.'

With trepidation Violet took the paper, seeing how intricately the note had been folded in on itself. Her name lay on the outside. She waited until her maid left to fossick around in her dressing room for the day's adornments.

Violet

It was written with a sharpened piece of charcoal from the fireplace in his room. Carefully she opened the missive so as not to tear the paper.

Thank you for your help. I will not forget it.

It was unsigned.

The hand was bold and sloped, the *f*'s tailed in a way that was foreign to an English way of writing. He'd underscored the word *not* as a means of empha-sising its importance and somehow she believed him, for he hadn't given the appearance of a man who might forget a promise.

Edith stepped back into the room, clothing across her arms and her expression full of curiosity. 'I don't know why he left so quickly, my lady, for the downstairs girl said there was blood on the handrail of the stair balustrade so he was hardly well.'

'Let us hope then that he got to his home safely and is being cared for by his own family as we speak.'

Even as she gave this platitude she wondered if he would have a family. He gave the impression of detachment and isolation, a man who had walked the harsher corners of the world and survived. Alone.

He'd been dressed as a gentleman and had spoken like one, too. Had she the way of his name she might have made enquiries, but she shook away such a thought. If he had wanted her to know him, he would have given it and when he had made a veiled reference about others who might have followed him she had sensed his preference to remain anonymous.

She had finally got her life back on track and she did not wish to derail her newly found contentment. Better to forget him. Better still, maybe, to have never stopped and picked him up in the first place, but she could not quite make herself believe in this line of reasoning. The snow outside today was thick and the temperatures had plummeted. If he had been left all night out in such conditions she doubted he would have been alive come the morning.

Later that evening, sitting with Amaryllis in the downstairs parlour, Violet tried to concentrate on the piece of embroidery she was doing of a rural scene with a thatched cottage near a river, the garden full of summer flowers before it. The fire was bright and warm, the embers sending out a good deal of heat.

Outside she could hear the occasional carriage passing, their noise muffled by at least four inches of newly fallen snow. Usually she loved this kind of quiet end to a winter day, with the darkness complete and a project in hand. Tonight, however, she was feeling restless and agitated.

'My lady's maid said that the marketplace was full of gossip this morning.' There was a certain tone to Amara's words that made her look up.

'Gossip?' Violet was not one to enjoy the whispers of tittle-tattle, but after her badly broken sleep she could not help but ask.

'It is being said that there was a fight last night in a boarding house in Brompton Place that left a man dead. A gentleman, too, by the sounds. Seems the man had his throat cut. Brutally.'

The hint of question in her sister-in-law's voice demanded an answer.

'And you think the stranger we brought home may have had something to do with this?'

'Well, we did find him at one end of Brompton Place and there was blood on his clothes, Violet. He also carried multiple weapons. God, he might have done away with us all in our beds had he the inclination for it and then where would we have been?'

Violet stopped the tirade as soon as she could. 'Did anyone in the marketplace have an idea of the dead man's name or occupation?'

'I do not think so. It is understood that he was from the city and that he had a gun found beside him and a full purse in his pocket.'

'It was not taken by whoever had killed him?'

'That's the way of it. It was violence the murderer was after, not the money, it seems. I suppose there are men here like that, men who live in the underbelly of London and in places we would have no knowledge of. Maybe he wanted to silence the other so that what was known between them should never be allowed to escape and it is a secret so terrible there will be repercussions everywhere.'

'I think you have been reading too many books, Amara. Perhaps it was simply an argument that got out of hand.'

A sniffle alerted her to stronger feelings. 'I feel scared, Violet, for an incident like this brings everything that much closer. What if they find out about us? What then? This could all happen again if we are not cautious.'

'It won't, I promise you. They will never find out.'

'I cannot pretend to be as brave as you are. I wish I could be, but I can't.'

'We are here in London, Amaryllis, and it has been over fifteen months since Harland died. We are safe.'

Violet laid the embroidery in her lap, all the neat and ordered rows of stitchery so contrary to the thoughts she was having. Did Amara hold the right of it? Had she fallen headlong into a world of disorder and tumult by rescuing a man she knew nothing at all about?

I will not *forget it.*

His note came to mind, too. Words of gratitude or of threat?

She had promised herself at the graveside of her late husband to be circumspect and prudent for that was the way that safety dwelled. And now look. Here she was wondering if the locks on her doors would be strong enough and if the stranger who knew exactly the layout of her house might be back.

Her contentment fell into disarray like a house built of cards, each argument falling on to the other until there was nothing left at all to find a truth with.

Stupid. Stupid, she chastised herself, her heart racing. She had been here before, in a position of weakness and vulnerability, a place she had promised never to be again. The worry inside knocked her off balance.

Swallowing hard, she made herself smile. It never paid to let anyone know your true feelings, for then control would be gone and this charade was all she had left of herself.

'I am sure the constable will find the culprit, Amara, and that shall be the very last we hear of it.'

'You do not think we ought to say anything about the one who was here last night? His wounds? The blood?'

'No, I don't think we should.' These words came with all the conviction she could muster and she was glad to see her sister-in-law nod in agreement.

He was most memorable. He would stand out in a crowd. The scar, the golden eyes, his beauty and his tallness. All the pieces of a man who was not in any way ordinary and so easy to find if someone was looking.

Danger balanced on the edge of a precipice, the beginnings of the consequences of her lies, the start of all that might come next? Another thought also occurred to her.

'Are the clothes the stranger wore last night still in the laundry?'

'No. They were dried early before the kitchen fire and the downstairs maid has ironed them.'

'Can you find them for me, Amara? Perhaps they might tell us things.'

'Things we may not wish to know?'

When Violet failed to answer, her sister-in-law stood and took her leave.

Why should she want to understand more about the stranger by gathering clues from his laundered garments? Could knowing more hurt her? With Harland she remembered sifting through his lies and truths and feeling sullied, a sort of panicked dirtiness inherent in every new thing she discovered about him.

When Amaryllis returned, she handed the items over with a heavy frown. 'If one made it one's business never to look into the hidden affairs of others, oblivion would be the result, Violet. Perhaps the curious hold a curse that trips them up repeatedly. I think we ought to donate these garments to charity and forget that we ever met this man. He is gone and it is for the best. For what it is worth, the butler said he had the look of duplicity about him and, of all the things in the world, we do not need that again.'

Then, after uttering a quick goodnight, her sister-in-law was gone, the door closed behind her. Violet was pleased to be alone with what was left of the man she'd found on the street, the fine linen of his shirtsleeves edged in silver and the breeches of a good quality serge. Lifting the material to her face, she breathed in, but the smell of him had disappeared. Only lye soap and fire smoke remained.

'Who are you?' she whispered into the night. 'And where are you now?'

The booming of a clock out in the hallway was her answer. He had faded into the teeming thousands who called London their home, lost in the melee of survival and danger. He would not be back.

Placing the garments on the small table beside her, she determined not to think of him again.

Chapter Two

Aurelian de la Tomber, Eighth Comte de Beaumont and heir to the Dukedom of Lorraine-Lillebonne, lay in a gilded bathtub in his rented town house on Portman Square, trying to block out the throbbing pain in his side.

The man who had jumped out at him in the darkness of the boarding house had meant business and it was only a last-second intuition that had made him duck to the left and catch a bullet in his arm rather than the full force of it through his chest. He'd slit his assailant's throat without blinking, his training homing in to demand full retribution. The fellow had gone down without a word, dead before he hit the floor, a fact that Lian deemed a shame given it would have been useful to have known who'd been sent to kill him.

The man's clothes had held some clue for they were the garments of a gentleman. Lian had found a purse full of gold when he had rifled through the jacket in the few moments he'd had before the alarm was raised and footsteps were heard. The chain about his neck had sported a St Christopher medallion. A travelling man, perhaps, or a superstitious one? The medallion had looked like a bauble of good quality silver.

He should have known it might come to this when he'd left France, for greed was a powerful deterrent to telling the truth and the monies sent by the supporters of Napoleon to those who might help them in England had been substantial.

What he had not expected was her. Lady Addington with her red hair and kind eyes, blessed with the sort of light shimmering all around that could expose every single demon within him.

He raised one hand and saw it shake, a froth of fine lavender soap across his skin. He'd been noticing these tremors more and more of late, just another side effect of the life he had lived.

'Dieu, aidez-moi.'

He remembered he'd sworn in French last night, too, a mistake that came from blood loss and dizziness. He seldom made such errors and cursed anew, the shifting exhaustion he'd felt for months lessening his usual caution.

Who the hell could have known that he was here in London on the sort of business that usually stayed secret and unheralded? What had happened after he had left the boarding house on Brompton Place?

He could remember very little of the previous night's attack, save for speaking to Lady Addington in a bedchamber when he'd been cleaned up and the doctor had left. The swelling in his side was greater this morning, the tight heat releasing into a throbbing ache. There were slight memories of sleet and cold and the sound of a carriage coming on as he fell, but that was about the most of it.

Would Lady Addington talk to the London law-keepers and give them his description? Would there be repercussions that might follow? He had no family here save for his younger sister and his two ageing aunts. A further worry that, for their safety was paramount in everything he did.

Violet Addington's freckles had been astonishing and her colouring had held the sort of vivid glowing richness that he could never before remember seeing and now could not forget.

She'd worn a diamond ring on the third finger of her left hand, but there had been no sign of a husband save for the portrait he'd caught sight of at the bottom of the stairs as he had left, the night light in the hall falling across the face of a man who was imposing and elegant. Her countenance was drawn beside his, a younger, more uncertain version of the woman she'd become.

Rising from the water, he took a towel from the rack and tied it about his waist, catching his reflection in the full-length mirror. He rarely looked at himself these days, but tonight he did. Tonight the scar on his chin was raised and red in the light and the new wound above his ear ate into the black of his hair. His chest was bandaged, hiding ruin's pathway across the skin, though the swollen bruising on his arm was visible.

His life was reflected in the hardness of his eyes

and in the deep lines that ran down each side of his face. Every year he'd worked for the Ministère de la Guerre had placed new scars upon him. The sabre cuts across his back, the many small knife wounds that ran over his hands and his lower arms, the missing half-finger resulting from the debacle with Les Chevaliers and his betrayal by Celeste Fournier-Shayborne.

He knew that the Addington servants must have seen such ruination upon him and wondered just what they might have relayed to their mistress. Or to a master?

The cross on plaited leather at his neck caught his attention next. Veronique. He'd taken it from her body after he'd pulled her out of the Seine and he'd never removed it. The remnants of lost chances and the aching brokenness of love. The beginning of his indifference, too.

A clean shirt hid most of the damage as he pulled it on, a pair of breeches following and then his boots. This double game of intelligence was taking his life piece by piece.

At any moment chaos could consume him. He felt it coming as a bleakness he could not control and then as a shaking that numbed all he knew to be good.

The images of Paris were there, too, of course, Henri Clarke's *ministère* and its constant and brutal violence. There was softness in small snatches at brothels and taverns filled with music, connections of the flesh that held only darkness and brevity.

Once he had been a good man. He'd believed in justice and equality and fairness. Once he had slumbered from dusk to dawn barely moving, his dreams quiet, graceful things without any of the monsters that now came calling as soon as he shut his eyes.

In the town house of Lady Addington he had slept the best he had in months. He could barely believe it when the clock in the corridor outside had struck out the hour of six and he had woken.

Three hours of straight and uninterrupted slumber. It was a record.

He knew he had to go back into society to complete his mission here, but she would recognise him now, would know his face. Would she be wise enough to keep quiet about their meeting in the middle of a cold London night? He didn't want her to be implicated. He didn't want her to be pulled into something he knew could hurt her.

But if she saw him unbidden? What might happen then? What if her servants talked? Or the driver of the Addington conveyance? Or the doctor with his clumsy hands? Even the plump housekeeper had watched him in a way that made him wonder.

Hell. He never took these risks at home, never walked through the streets of Paris compromised by mistake. He was getting old and soft, that was the trouble. Thirty-four years were upon him already and, he wondered, would he even manage thirty-five?

The wound at his side pulled as he turned too fast and he placed his arm hard against the pain, containing it and keeping it in. He'd need to lay low for a week at least to gather strength, but after that he meant to find those who had ordered his demise. Find them and deal with them. He had his leads and his hunches in the art of intelligence had always served him well.

After his father came to England, they would never return to France. There would be no more favours, no more final turn of the dice for a regime he'd long since stopped believing in. He would live on his estate in the ordered greenness of Sussex.

Compton Park.

The remodelling had been finished for a good ten months now and yet he had barely spent a night there. He wanted that to change. He needed a base so that all the parts of him that were compromised did not spin out, never to be regathered again. Lost in artifice and trickery.

He needed light.

That thought had him swearing because the only woman he had ever met with a distinct aura of brightness was Lady Addington and she was probably rueing her decision to pick him up off the freezing streets to take him home.

Such rumination made him feel dizzy and he sat with relief on the leather chair in his dressing room, a drink in hand and trying to regain a balance that could allow his breath to soften.

He could do nothing yet. He needed to get stronger, needed the weakness that held him captive to dissipate and to lessen. Wisdom came with the knowing of when to wait and when to strike and at this moment he understood that his physical means were restricted.

Drawing in, he made himself relax, made himself reach for the remembered warmth of a Parisian summer, the music in the streets of Montmartre, the pastries in the small bakeries off St Germaine. The lazy flow of the Seine was there, too, in his mind's eye, wending its easy way through the city, as were the ancient mellow buildings of the Marais with its hidden spaces and green trees. The history of life wound about his uncertainty, knitting resolve and purpose together.

His thumb rubbed across the engraving on his ring which evoked the traditions of an ancient and powerful family. Such rituals heartened him and rebuilt the shaken foundations of his hurt.

Lord, how many are my foes.
How many rise up against me…

David's Prayer of Deliverance had helped him many times and he liked the peace of it. Finishing the entreaty and the last of his drink he leaned back against leather and closed his eyes. To rest, not to sleep. He'd long since given up even the hope of that.

Six nights later Summerley Shayborne, Viscount Luxford, was at his door.

'This is unexpected.' Aurelian could barely take in his friend's presence.

'Celeste insisted I come up to see you, Lian. She felt there was something wrong.'

'Has your wife become a clairvoyant now? A woman who might see through space and time?'

'More like a pregnant and anxious worrier. She has

constant inklings of imminent danger about those who are close to her and sends me to check.'

Aurelian smiled. Shay's wife might have been the reason for the scar on his chin and the missing half-finger but there was a lot of respect between them now. He liked Celeste Shayborne, loved her even, if he were to be honest, like a favoured sister or cousin.

'I am fine.'

He suddenly remembered uttering those very words when first Violet Addington had leaned over him on the street, the clouds above her filled with snow. A new memory, that. He filed it away to think about later.

'Hawkins said that you were lucky to escape with your life. Your valet said a bullet that went through your arm and side festered and it was only the ministrations and expertise of your old aunt's physician that stood between you and death.'

'Hawkins talks too much.'

'Your valet is the cousin of mine. He feels he is family and kin looks after its own.'

Family. Shay had always been like that to him, the brother he'd never had and a friend who through thick and thin had stuck beside him.

'Someone is trying to kill me, Shay.'

'Hell.'

'Someone sent a note to meet at the boarding house at Brompton Place. My assailant shot me the moment I arrived, missing anything important inside by a hair's breadth.'

'Had you seen him before?'

'No, but he was well dressed and had a heavy purse in his jacket pocket.'

'When you first arrived in England two weeks ago, you said that you were here to recover some lost gold. Someone might be more than interested in stopping you from doing that.'

Lian crossed the room and found two glasses and his best bottle of brandy. Proceeding to pour out generous drinks, he motioned Shay to take a seat in a chair by the fire and, when he did so, took the opposite one himself.

'Interested because ill-gotten gains can make men do a lot of things that they might not otherwise countenance?'

'Like shoot a man in cold blood?'

He smiled. 'That, too. Those in Paris who sent the gold to England in the first place now want it back, for it seems that their plans of a rebellion against the English way of life has come to nothing.'

'That's what this is about? Napoleon languishes at Elba. They can't possibly think to keep his hopes of conquering Europe again alive.'

'There were six substantial shipments of gold sent in the hopes of inciting insurgence. They stopped fourteen months ago.'

'Shipments to whom?'

'That's the problem. Whoever received the gold was careful to hide their identity, but a small statue was sent anonymously to Paris warning against dispatching more. The gold marks on the piece had been tampered with and the bust consisted mostly of silver and lead.'

'A way to hide the missing gold should anyone ask after it?'

'Precisely. The jeweller who I am led to believe fashioned the piece is away from London until the week after next and has left no mention of his travel intentions. When I see him perhaps then there will be some answers.'

'Leaving you as the one visible person trying to shed light on a world of greed?'

This time Lian laughed. 'Everyone is expendable. You of all people would know that, Shay.'

'Then get out. Come south to Sussex and stop. Settle down at Compton Park and become another man, a happier one, just as I have. Leave the gold alone and allow others to die for its recovery.'

Shay's advice was so like the hope he had just been ruminating on that Lian felt the rip of it in his heart. 'My father is still in Paris.'

'So if you were to defect now he would be at risk?'

'Precisely.'

He liked talking with Shay. He liked his honest astuteness. He liked that the shadows others never saw were so much part of what they both knew. It made the truth easy.

He could see the thoughts racing in his friend's eyes and knew the moment when the tumblers clicked into place.

'You've been made the damn bait for all of this?'

'Yes.'

'And you think you can win against everyone in a city that you no longer know well?'

'It's still possible. These people are sometimes like amateurs who are easy to gain the measure of.'

'The other night did not sound so easy. Who the hell was it that rescued you, then?'

Lian gritted his teeth together and shook his head. He should have known that this would be the next question.

'Lady Addington, a widow from Chelsea, brought me back to her home. I have found out since that she was married to Viscount Addington, a minor aristocrat from the north. She came down here to London after the death of her husband.'

'Addington? The name is familiar although I cannot quite place it.'

'A statue identical to the one that turned up in Paris sat on the mantel of her downstairs salon.'

The shock of that statement settled for a moment into the silence, vibrating into question.

'So Violet Addington knew you would be there? On that particular street after midnight? She is involved?'

'I hope not.'

'Why?'

'I'd be long dead if she had not picked me up out of the gutter. I think I owe her something for it.'

Shay started to laugh. 'There's more, by God, for you don't even sound like yourself. Work was always strictly professional for you and damned be anyone who got in the way.'

'That was when I believed in Napoleon's ability

to make France a better place. Then I didn't and your own wife was a part of that. When she exposed me in Paris I understood that there was no true loyalty left and the idea of spilling one's blood for nothing was less appealing.'

'I still have contacts, Lian. Good ones, too. Perhaps…'

'No. Your loyalties now lie with your family, with Celeste and Loring and the new little one when it comes. I can handle this.'

'Wounded and alone?'

'I am improving daily. This morning I managed the stairs without holding on to the banister. Tomorrow I will climb them twice.'

'Someone knows you are here and if they are prepared to kill you without any dialogue at all, then everyone is dangerous. You have to promise me that you'll send word if you need help.'

Lian nodded, but knew that only if he lay dying would he consider it and he did not intend for that to happen. His more usual manner was reasserting itself, the ideas churning and the details noticed. It was a jigsaw, intelligence, all the pieces needing to be put in just the right place. Talking to Shay had steadied him and made him think. He would need to go back to see Violet Addington and ask her about the statue.

He dreaded her answer.

When the conversation turned to other things, Aurelian relaxed. It was good to have a friend to talk with.

'How is Celeste's grandmother?'

'Flourishing as she hurls advice and gives her

opinion on any and everything related to bringing up children.'

'Yet her own were such disappointments.'

'Well, Celeste says that a second chance is what everybody needs and she is going to give it with love to Susan Joyce.'

'You were lucky in her, Shay. Lucky to have found her.'

'And don't I know it.'

Fiddling with his glass, Lian leaned back in the wing chair, the ancient leather squeaking.

'When did you realise that she was the one, the one you loved? The one you could not live without.'

'About a moment after I met her again in Paris in heavy disguise and whispering sensitive state secrets. Why do you want to know that?'

Lian looked down, careful to shade his eyes. Shay was a man who noticed almost as much as he did and it was always the tiny gestures that gave one away.

'Sometimes it is good to hear about things that are not hard or wrong or dangerous.'

'Does Lytton Staines know you are back?'

'I haven't seen him yet, but then I have not been here for long. He is due back from Scotland tomorrow.'

'My advice would be to go out on the town with him when you are better, for in a social setting you can observe Lady Addington without being noticed. See who she converses with. Find out those who might also be involved and get your leads there. If you are going to be the lure in all of this, you may as well go slowly and carefully so that what's just happened to you never does so again. Where was the gold sent to here in England?'

'To a man who went by the name of Derwent in Kensington. I followed up that lead and can find no sign that he ever existed.'

'A front, then?'

'The investors in Paris received acknowledgement of the donations. They also received correspondence outlining detailed plans of connecting with others who were anti-government here. Then communication simply stopped about a year and a half ago.'

'It took you a while to get here, then?'

'Those sending the gold were all gentlemen. They did not wish to be identified publicly with such an endeavour, preferring to make it a more private crusade.'

'What changed?'

'When the statue turned up with the warning they thought that blackmail might come next.'

'And because you were half-English and had been to school here you were chosen as the one to come and sort it all out?'

'Not quite. After your wife's accusations against me in Paris I have been watched, though *distrusted* might even be a better word for it. When I was shot in the boarding house on Brompton Place I even wondered if the man was not French.'

'God. A double-cross? Le Ministère de la Guerre?'

'The struggle for power is never easy. People do not wish to relinquish their assets without a fight.'

'And one of those assets is you?'

Lian began to laugh and felt better. It had been a

long time since he had been able to speak so openly like this.

'I got out the money I had in France a good while ago after selling my personal properties.'

'Which was another black mark to your name?'

'I suppose so. Being the first to recognise the truth of Napoleon's doomed campaigns and act upon it leaves others…vengeful. The noble families are not what they once were in France, for although aristocracy is tolerated it is no longer encouraged. Papa sent my sister and his old aunts here to England when he sensed the danger in it all, but nothing could induce him to leave.'

'So he stayed?'

'My mother's grave is at Vernon. That was part of it, too. His heart lies in that soil.'

'The soft underside of true politics? The place where the soul collides with reason?'

'Perhaps.'

'So your first questions will be to Lady Addington.'

He nodded, hating to have her name so carelessly tossed into the ring. 'She is scared somehow and isolated. When she speaks there are shadows in her words.'

'How long were you in her house?'

'Four hours and I slept for three of them.'

Shay finished his brandy and got up to pour himself another. 'She made quite an impression on you, then, for such a brief acquaintance.'

'There were many books in French in the downstairs library, though the whole place looked shabby and in need of redecoration.'

'The twin persuasions of loyalty and greed.'

'But that's not enough, is it? I need a reason. She is a lady and a gentlewoman. She is delicate and thin. Her hands are soft. Her heart is kind.'

'The husband, then? Lord Addington? How did he die?'

'In an accident in the Addington stables. One of his prize stallions booted him.'

'Were there witnesses?'

'None.'

'Easy to apply such a death, then, if you had the motivation. Enough gold might give you that.'

'There's something else, too.' He waited until Shay returned again before beginning.

'Violet Addington's father, Wilfred Bartholomew, was a northern businessman made rich by his acquisition of jewellery shops.'

'A man who knew his way around gold, then, and how to stretch its worth.'

'And his sister left England years ago to marry a Frenchman and settle in Lyon. A family connection?'

Shay stood against the warmth of flame. 'I miss it sometimes, Lian, all the energy of intelligence. I miss it until I kiss my wife and son and understand the impossibility of ever inviting danger to arrive again at my hearth.'

Lian knew exactly what it was he spoke about. 'When I get out I will be like you and never look back. It will be a relief.'

'Then do it soon, for you appear as if you have not slept well for a year.'

'That's probably because I haven't.'

'Here's to Lady Addington, then, a woman who fills you with light and sleep.'

Chapter Three

⸻⸻⸱⸻⸻

The music was the 'Duke of Kent's Waltz'. Violet had always hated the piece and she gritted her teeth together to try to block out the anger inside that arose unbidden. The country-dance tune had been the one she had been playing on her small piano at Addington Manor when Harland had found out her father's will had left him all the Bartholomew wealth and he reasoned he no longer needed to be conciliatory.

She'd dressed with care tonight, though her ancient green high-necked gown was plain. Harland would have loathed it because it did nothing to dampen down her vivid colouring and consume some of the flame. She remembered her husband wrapping her hair around his fist and pulling her into him, not in gentleness but in a burning anger.

'Stop showing yourself like you do, Violet. Stop being brazen. You are no longer a simple commoner, but the wife of a viscount. Act like it.'

Tonight she had caught the length of her tresses up

and added a turban to hide them, though there was no help for the fire-flamed tendrils that kept escaping around her face.

'Your hair is reminiscent of the shade a street prostitute might favour.' Harland had let her know of all the connotations of the colour after their marriage and for the first few years she had taken to dyeing it a dark brown.

Since coming out of an enforced mourning a few months ago, she'd often worn bright hues, six years of anonymity enough of a punishment for any woman with sense. But she had yet to release her hair from the confines of habit and thus the turban had stayed.

'Violet.' The call of her name had her turning and a friend, Lady Antonia MacMillan, caught at her arm. 'I've been waiting an age for you to come and thought you must have decided to stay home.'

'I was at the Wilsons' ball for the early part of the evening and did not realise the lateness of the hour.'

Amara had taken herself off to sit along the side of the room. Violet thought she would join her after talking with Antonia. Tonight she felt tired and a bit restless. It had been over two weeks since rescuing her stranger from the frozen street and she thought he might have contacted her somehow. But he hadn't.

'Well, I am so glad you have arrived for you need to catch sight of the Comte de Beaumont. He has most recently returned from Paris and has set the *ton* alight. There are, of course, a few whispers of his past which only help to make him more...alluring.'

'Whispers?' She smiled at the theatrical voice Antonia used.

'He was once heartbroken. His young wife drowned.'

The sadness of such a thing washed across Violet. For young lovers to be parted for ever by such adversity was shocking, though a little piece of her also thought if Harland had been snatched away by ill fortune in the first month of their marriage she would have remembered him with far more fondness.

'He is tall, handsome and clever and I have been doing my very best to catch his eye all evening, but to no avail whatsoever...'

Such words produced a wariness and she hoped that Antonia would not throw herself at the man in her company. She was here at the Creightons' ball for the light conversation and not for the machinations of attraction, so when Mr Douglas Cummings crossed the floor to ask her for the next dance, Violet assented.

Cummings was a man who sorely needed a woman to boost his morale and confidence and a shudder went through her. Once she had been that sort of a wife to Harland.

The anger that sat close made her breathe in deeply. It was why she came to these soirées night after night and stayed late into the early mornings so that when she reached her home and her bed she would be weak with exhaustion and would sleep. Dreamless.

She was thinner than she had been in years, the generous curves that her husband had delighted in at first now lessened. A changed and altered appearance; but it was the inside she truly worried about, for there were weeks when she felt empty save for an all-consuming fury.

It was on the third turn of the room dancing in the arms of Mr Douglas Cummings that she saw him, standing over against the wall and surrounded by people. She felt her footing falter.

'Are you quite well? We can sit this dance out should you wish it.' Cummings's words held question.

'No, it was only a misstep.'

Her voice sounded off even to her own ears, but she wanted to pass by again to make sure that it was truly her mysterious stranger and the best way to do this was by using the waltz.

She tried to smile and concentrate, on Cummings, on the dance steps, on her heartbeat that sounded louder and louder in her ears. Then he was in sight again, twenty feet away, speaking with a woman whose hand rested in a daring fashion across his chest.

There was no sign at all of the wound above his right ear. Tonight his hair was *en queue*, tightly tied back, and was much longer than anyone here wore theirs. He looked different from the man who had been pale and drawn and trussed up in a nightgown in her house.

He looked magnificent.

Who was he?

As though she had spoken out loud he looked up and their gazes caught across the space. Shocking. Unfathomable. For the first time in a long, long while

Violet felt her body rouse into heat. Breaking the contact, she turned back to her dancing partner.

'There are many people here tonight, almost a crush.' If each word held a quiver, Cummings had the good grace not to comment upon it.

'It's the speciality of the Creightons. Invite anybody and everybody and hope that in the mix there is scandal and mayhem. They thrive on it and it is why the invites are so sought after.'

'A dangerous logic?'

'And yet everyone turns up because it is mesmerising to see the risk of chaos in action.'

Her head felt light and she clutched at Cummings's hand more tightly than she meant to. Would there be some repercussion this evening to the man with the scar on his chin? Were there others here tonight who might know of the fracas in the boarding house on Brompton Place? More than a fracas. A murder. Over two weeks ago now which could indicate some sense of safety?

She did not recognise any of the men who stood in the group around him. The ladies were some of the most beautiful women of the *ton* and the ones whose reputations were not quite solid. The stranger gave off the same sort of air, one of danger and risk and plain pure sexuality. The connection shocked her.

'I think perhaps I might sit down now, Mr Cummings, if you do not mind.'

When she peered back at the group in the corner she saw that his interest had once again been taken by the woman beside him and he was laughing at something she'd said, the lines in his cheeks deeply etched.

Dismissed and forgotten. Perhaps he truly did not recognise her or perhaps he did and wanted no reminder of that particular peculiar evening. Both possibilities left her with no avenue of further discourse.

Antonia swept into view beside her even as Violet sat.

'Did you see the French Comte? You must have noticed him. He is over by the pillars at the far side of the room?'

'Who?' An inkling as to just what Antonia was going to say raced through reason.

'The Comte de Beaumont, of course. The man I was telling you of. I saw you looking at him so do not say you weren't. Is he not just the most divine creature you have ever laid your eyes on?'

Her stranger was the Comte de Beaumont? The man recently come into English society and sending all its ladies into swoons?

Such a realisation was shocking, but beneath this truth other things were solidifying. He was unmatched, but he was also full of a darkness that could only hurt her.

'My brother said he saw him going into one of the wicked opium dens in town. To partake, do you think?' The shock in Antonia's eyes was underlined by excitement.

Harland had used laudanum in the last years of his life, too, as an aid to his gambling losses, the sickly-sweet smell still inclined to make her feel ill. The dream weaver, he had called it, as he'd tried to foist it upon her.

'It might loosen you up, Violet. You used to be so much more fun than you are now.'

He had said other things, too; an undertone of bitter recrimination in each and every word.

With determination she pulled her thoughts back to this minute, the gentle three-point melody of a waltz in the distance and the chandeliers above twinkling in long lines of muted light. The beauty and energy of the room swirled around her. Here nothing sordid or ignoble could touch her. Here she was beyond reproach and lauded.

The vanity of such a thought worried her, but she tossed that aside.

Could the Comte de Beaumont have murdered a man a few moments before she'd found him? There had been blood on the blade in his boot and much more on his clothes.

'The Frenchman is a man of secrets, would you not say, for there are whispers that in Paris his family escaped the Terror unscathed and are rich beyond imagination.'

'Anything can be said of anyone, Antonia, yet that does not make it true.'

Her friend smiled. 'Still, is there not something about him, Violet? Some tempting beauty? Lady Catherine Osborne obviously thinks so, for look how she hangs on to him as if she might never let him go.'

Making no effort to turn in that direction, Violet

wished that her friend would show the same sort of reserve.

'His mother was English. One of the Forsythes from Essex, although she passed away a good few years ago in France. His father is still hale and hearty. Duc de Lorraine-Lillebonne is his title as he hails from that ancient family.'

Lineage and wealth. No wonder the Comte was being fêted by all the women of the *ton*. But why then had she found him lying wounded on the side of a cold and midnight road, a man who had given her no name by which to place him?

Secrets. They hung across his shoulders like a heavy mantle; she could see it in the way he held himself and in the quiet watchfulness of his person. Perhaps it took one to know one, she also thought, wondering if her own mistruths were so very easily noted.

The sound of the orchestra tuning up for another dance caught at her attention and she smiled. The quadrille. More usually on any given night her dance card would have been full, but because she had been so late in arriving this evening she had not even taken it out of her reticule. She was pleased that she hadn't, for it meant she could leave earlier and without comment.

Antonia knocked at her arm. 'De Beaumont is coming this way with my brother. Smile, Violet, for you have the grimace of one marching to her death instead of feasting your eyes and appreciating true masculine beauty.'

Gregory MacMillan was all eagerness as he reached

them. 'Comte de Beaumont, may I present my sister, Lady Antonia MacMillan, and her great friend Lady Addington. The Comte is recently come from Paris and has asked me for an introduction to the two most beautiful women in the room.'

When Violet looked up she could see that the flowery words of Antonia's brother were just that. The Comte de Beaumont looked as surprised by the sentiment as she had been.

'I am pleased to meet you both.'

So that is how he wished to play it, the recent history between them discounted. With a small tip of her head she noticed that Antonia was doing her very best to crawl up against the newcomer. 'I do hope that you are enjoying your sojourn to London, Comte?'

The flirtatiousness in her tone made Violet wince.

Please, God, she thought, *let this finish.* Let him move away before the dancing begins in earnest. Let him tip his head and leave us behind.

'It is a city I do not know well any more, I am afraid, Lady Antonia. A city of contrasts.'

Dangerous and bustling. Lies and truth. Gunshots and dancing. Coyness and peril. Life and death. Love and hate. Light and darkness.

He did not now exhibit any semblance of pain or discomfort and the scar across his chin looked almost pale, lost in the dim light of candelabras.

But Antonia had not finished with all her questions. 'I have heard you have bought a house in Sussex, my lord, and a very fine one by all accounts.'

'Indeed. I was down south for a few weeks last year and purchased it on a whim.'

A whim?

The Comte de Beaumont did not look like a man who ever acted upon whims. Light and fancy things, whims. When he saw Violet smile at such a musing his eyes darkened.

'Would you like to dance, Lady Addington? I think I can just about remember the steps of the quadrille.'

She could not refuse under such close perusal, though Antonia did not look pleased at all.

Within a moment he had shepherded her on to the floor, the touch of his good arm burning into her back. When they stood to face each other she was lost for words.

'Thank you.' His voice was low and quiet.

For the lie? For the dance? For not calling in at the Home Office and telling them her story in detail? For standing there and pretending she did not know him? For rescuing him from certain death on a frozen night?

'You are welcome.'

Here was not the place for more with the cream of the *ton* present, as their love of gossip and scandal could ruin him. Violet wondered if de Beaumont held a knife in his pocket even under the lights and among the rustle of silk. She decided that he must.

'You have made quite an impression in society since arriving in England, Comte de Beaumont. Everyone is talking of you and you have not been here long.'

'A daunting thing that, Lady Addington, given our circumstances.'

'I received your note.' She whispered this, just in case.

'And I meant every word on it.'

She felt the tightening of his fingers against her hand, a small and hidden communication. Barely there.

'Why?'

Suddenly she no longer wanted to be so careful. If he had murdered a man the other week he was not someone she should encourage. But then again if he hadn't...

'When someone saves your life there is a debt owed.'

'And when someone takes a life it is just the same.'

'Touché,' he whispered as the dance pulled them apart into the arms of others.

When he returned she felt a giddy sense of place, but firmly squashed it down as his arms linked with her own.

'Do you try to make yourself unattractive, Lady Addington?'

She nearly missed her step.

'The turban does not suit you. Neither does the gown.'

The shock of such an unexpected and personal remark ran through her unchecked. 'My dressmaker would be distraught.'

'How old is the woman?'

'Pardon?'

'The female who fashions your garments? What is her age?'

Violet frowned, thinking of how hard she had worked all week to modify her ancient gown with her lady's maid to make it presentable. She had never been offered a budget for clothing when she had been married and now even making ends meet was hard. Harland's heavy gambling had all but ruined them, the town house the only thing as his widow she had been able to save unencumbered. There had certainly not been enough left for a refurbishment or for new gowns.

'I think you should hardly be—'

He interrupted her.

'Tell her to find a dark blue velvet and to slash down both the neckline and the sleeves. More is not always better,' he added and she saw a definite twinkle in his eyes.

'The Parisian love of decadence might not suit the British mentality.'

'And you think the Puritan look does? Look around you. Others show much more than an inch of skin. You are still a woman beneath the heavy serge and one with gentle curves. I felt them when you helped me up from the frozen street.'

'A gentleman does not mention such things, sir.'

'Yet it seems to me you need to hear them, my lady. You are hiding yourself and I am wondering why?'

This sort of conversation was one she was unpractised at, though the tone of it was exhilarating.

'Is every young lord in Paris tutored in this art of shallow flattery?'

'I wasn't at school in France.'

'Oh.' She was surprised by his answer.

'I went to Eton and then on to Oxford. A proper English upbringing with all my manners minded.'

'But then you left. You went home again?'

'Home,' he repeated, 'is often not where one expects it to be.'

'You talk in riddles, my lord, and I comprehend that your dancing style is so much more proficient than my own. Do not ask me to stand up with you again because I shall refuse.'

'Because you would worry about the opinions of those around you?'

'Oh, indeed I would, sir. If you do not realise that, then you fail to know me at all.'

'A disappointing honesty.'

'And there are so many more of them.'

'Violet.'

'Yes.' She jumped at his informal use of her name.

'Stop talking and dance with me.'

When he pulled her closer and his arms led her into steps she had never before learned she wondered if perhaps he was a magician making gold from clay, making flame from ashes.

'Will you be in London for long, Comte de Beaumont?' She asked this as the music slowed a few moments later.

'I hope not.'

'You will return to Paris, then?'

'No.'

Her effort at small talk faltered back into silence

and on the final flourish of the violin he dropped her hand and bowed at her solemnly. Then he was gone.

Violet found Antonia with two of her other friends and joined their small group. She would have simply liked to have walked to the door and left, to have found her carriage and retreated from the battle. For that is exactly what this meeting had felt like. As it was, she would need to wait for Amara's return from wherever it was she had disappeared to because she knew there would be questions otherwise.

It seemed that any conversation with the unknowable French Count always spiralled into uncertainty. She felt the anger of him, too, the hidden man under the urbanity of the more public one. His hands were not soft. They were the hands of one who had toiled and worked hard. He smelt of both brandy and lavender, the two scents combining into a wholly masculine flavour.

His sense of humour worried her the most. She knew that he watched her for she caught his glance across the room and hurriedly looked away.

What could he want? What did she? She wished suddenly that they might have met in the park, sheltered by the greenery from the eyes of others. And then what?

Lord, what was happening to her? For six years she had been frozen into shame and woodenness, any sense of the intimate pushed away firmly and resolutely. Yet just with one small dance it was as if a dam had been breached, allowing life to begin again, to green and blossom.

Le Comte de Beaumont probably had not even re-alised he was doing it. He was a man who would be overrun with feminine company, a male who would understand exactly his effect on the opposite sex.

She was twenty-seven years old, after all, and not a debutante filled with hopes and fantasy. She frowned, remembering Harland. He had swept her off her feet within a month and she had never thought to ques-tion all the things that did not quite add up about him.

Well, here was another man where nothing about him truly made sense. A wealthy foreign aristocrat in London and looking for what? He had said that he would not be here long and yet he had purchased a place in Sussex? A further question. The top portion of the third finger on his right hand was missing, a scar attesting to the injury.

A man of war, she thought, but not a soldier.

The settle of coldness within her began to build just as a shout of anger and challenge rang out from his direction.

'You think that you can get away with this, you French bastard, just walk in here and have society at your feet?'

The shorter fellow standing before de Beaumont had pulled himself right up into the Comte's face and had raised his voice in a threatening manner.

'You are more than inebriated, sir, and most irritat-ing with it. Perhaps you should go away?' These words were strained and less than flattering, the Comte's ac-cent all perfect English privilege and wealth.

But the other man was not backing off, whether by

reason of hard liquor or of poor judgement, and she watched him raise his fist and slam it directly into the mouth of the Frenchman.

A general gasp emanated all around them and there was a skittering as those in the burst of violence rushed out of the way, the exodus bringing her in closer to the action. It was easy to see the fury on de Beaumont's face.

Another assailant spun into the fracas, but the Comte simply caught his hand and twisted it, the aggressor screaming in pain. Then everything disintegrated as further punches were thrown. Suddenly the whole side at this end of the room seemed to be involved in a brawling fight.

This would never have happened in any other social situation of the *ton*, but those here this evening were a varied lot and the chance of a fight seemed to be exactly what they were waiting for.

De Beaumont looked more than at home and he was a most proficient adversary, for he shook off his assailants while barely breaking a sweat.

Violet shouted out a warning as a further man came from behind him, but already Antonia was pulling at her arm.

'Come, Violet. It is dangerous to be so close. There is no sense here—'

She did not finish, for there was the crash of a body hard against their own and then dizziness. When Violet put her hand up to her head she felt a sizeable lump and she straightened her silk turban with shaking fingers.

The room stood still, a slow-motion dance of eyes turning, the floating yellow fabric ballooned against each wall strange and blurring. Sound seemed diminished and distant and she was having difficulty in breathing.

Tilting her head, she saw the Comte watching her, blood on his lip and fury in his eyes. Then Antonia grabbed at her and lead her away.

'Are you hurt, Violet? My goodness, I have never in my whole life seen such a terrible thing.'

Her head ached and she was dizzy, but she did not wish to make a fuss. Amara was at her side now, too, shaking her head.

'We should not have come here—I knew it. The Creightons have little taste and even less sense. We should leave straight away.'

With a ringing in her ears and a feeling of nausea rising, Violet did just as they both wanted her to and turned for the door.

The French Comte had disappeared and she thought that he would just have to take his chances even with a recent bullet wound to the side. Only a few weeks had passed since his being almost dead and she imagined that he might have had the sense to lie low and recover. The beautiful woman he had been attached to was nowhere to be seen, either, so perhaps they had both left together? That realisation was surprisingly hurtful and she quickly shook it away.

Violet awoke in her room just as the clock outside in the hallway struck three. The Comte de Beaumont sat on the chair beside the bed, watching her. Surprisingly, she felt in no danger at all.

'I am sorry for what happened tonight.'

Violet held up her hand as though to stop any apology.

'How did you get in?'

'Your locks are very flimsy. It would be safer to have them changed.'

Ignoring that, she sat up further. The evening before had been like a small window into the life of a man for whom violence was a common theme and she could scarcely believe that he was here. 'Who are you?'

'Aurelian de la Tomber. My friends call me Lian.'

'And am I that? A friend?'

'You tried to help me a few hours ago. Why?'

'Help you?' She was stalling for time and he knew it.

'By calling out. By warning me. By involving yourself in something you should not have.'

'Because you are dangerous?'

'Completely.' One word ground out slowly. One word that didn't seem quite so English now. 'And you got wounded because of it.'

His tone seemed more grave than the small bruise on her skull should have elicited and she smiled. 'I am sure that I shall live. The doctor said it was a tiny injury.'

'Perhaps so this time, but why is no one here with you? Watching you? It cannot be safe to be alone after a knock to the head…'

She stopped him by asking another question.

'What did those men want with you?'

Shrugging, he leaned forward. 'The world of London society is a rarefied one, Lady Addington. All pomp and circumstance, but often lies, as well. A public debacle is probably one way of discrediting me or at least starting rumours.'

'Rumours?'

'That I am not solid. That demons stalk me. That trust in my motives might be misdirected. Were I now on the other side of such a ruse I might even say it was creditable.'

'You are not reassuring me on the merits of your true character with such talk. Why would they be trying to discredit you in the first place?'

'I am a stranger and our countries are at war. Your husband was a viscount from the north, was he not?'

She stayed silent, shocked by such a quick change in subject. Had he been finding out about her?

'Harland Addington was an upright man, according to many, though there are those who might say otherwise.'

'Otherwise?'

'There are whispers, my lady, that are…less flattering.'

'Are you threatening me, Monsieur le Comte?

'With such a small and private warning, Lady Addington? Hardly.'

The double meaning of his last rejoinder made her stiffen as he carried on explaining.

'It seems the Viscount's death was barely recorded

by many. The funeral was a small one. Some say his wife might have even been relieved?'

'Grief is a private thing. No one can know the very extent of another's sorrow.'

'Relief is the same. And retribution? Have you ever been to Paris?'

Her head began to throb, the bandage tightening over the drumbeat. Could he know some of the things she had found out about Harland? Or were these queries just conversational, almost languid, each hiding a wealth of knowledge?

'Is Douglas Cummings a man you know well, Lady Addington?' His tone was sharper now, less laconic. 'You held his hand most tightly in the dance.'

The constant change of subject set her off balance and worried her. 'I know him mostly because he works at the Home Office along with an old family friend, Mr Charles Mountford. Cummings is one of the secretaries there and has an unblemished reputation.'

He laughed then, softly. 'It is a rare man who lives his life without complaint or criticism.'

'I am not certain I understand you, Comte de Beaumont.'

'Do you truly not, my lady?'

She felt the blood leave her face as her mouth formed a denial, but he was already standing.

'Can you tell me how you came by the gold statue sitting on the mantel in your downstairs salon?'

'I do not know which one you mean. There is a large collection of art in that room, for Harland held a taste of beautiful things.'

She felt her skin blanch, the blood draining away in shock at the unintended double meaning of her words, but when she did not speak further he smiled in a way that was almost sad, his fingers lifting to twist the heavy ring off one finger.

'This is in repayment for your help.' He set the piece down on her bedside table. 'Buy yourself a ticket to somewhere far away from here for at least a month and disappear. It will be safer.'

'For you or for me?'

'For both of us, perhaps.' Reaching forward, he took her hand, placing a kiss on the opened palm. She felt his warmth and the roughness of stubble on her skin and leaned in to it. Then he was no longer there.

Could he know of her connection with the French gold and, more important, if he did, what would he do about it? Why had Aurelian de la Tomber appeared out of nowhere with his insinuations and his questions and his hard and desperate beauty?

The ring was heavy when she lifted it, his warmth still imbued in the metal. Tipping it into the light, she saw the punched stamps inside were readable despite the age of the piece. The flower marks of Paris indicated the purity of the carats and a crowned and scripted letter gave a date. Seventeen forty-five or forty-six, she guessed, and ran her finger across the maker's mark. A faded *V* in a circle.

Her father's jewellery business had led her to an interest in gold. She had always seen the beauty and age of its handcraft as the gift of an ancient art. A mark of responsibility, too, and a true establishment of location and worth. In her shifting world of blame and guilt such things seemed unearthly pure and unchangeable, the one permanent truth in a world of deceit.

She no longer trusted anyone. Even herself, for in the conversation with Aurelian de la Tomber in the darkness she had wanted to reach out and touch him, to keep him safe and unharmed. She'd wanted much more than that, too, if she was truly honest, but those thoughts were better left alone.

She would need to change the locks on all her doors for sturdier ones if the Comte de Beaumont could so easily access her town house.

Leaving London and running was out of the question. She had not faced her problems before and because of it nothing had ever changed or improved. This time she needed to be present and certain. This time she would cower to no one.

With care, she reached over and rang the bell on the other side of her bed and waited until the maid came in.

'Send up a footman to me first thing in the morning, please, Edith. I need to have something delivered promptly and safely.'

'Yes, my lady. Mrs Hamilton said I was to wake her if you stirred…'

'Pretend I did not and go to bed yourself. I have no need of company until the morrow.'

When the door shut, she pushed back the covers and sat on the side of her bed until she felt the dizziness lessen. After another moment or so she stood to walk to her writing desk. Extracting paper and pen and a book to press on, she scurried back to the warmth of the blankets.

She gave no heading to the missive, but carried straight on into the body of her message. A direct and ordered reply leaving the receiver with no doubt of her intentions. It was how she managed things these days, it was how she survived.

When she'd finished, she tucked the ring into a twist of paper and laid both items on her side table.

Would this set some dreadful chain of events into motion or had she just stopped the cogs of an imminent disaster from winding up further?

'Unlike you, Harland,' she whispered into the dark, 'I take responsibility for my actions and am prepared to bear the consequences.'

The letter came before the hour of nine, an unusual happenstance in the ordered world of the *ton*. A servant of the Addingtons had delivered the note personally and when Aurelian opened the missive he could well see why.

The ancient ring of the Lorraine-Lillebonne family seat was twisted up in the protection of paper and with it came a message.

Either you have no idea of the value of this ring, my lord, or the promise of my silence must be of inordinate worth to you. Whichever it is, my honour is not for sale.

She hadn't signed it, but when he brought the parchment to his nose Lian could smell her. Violets. He smiled. Well, the game was started and the players had already surprised him. He liked that they had. The feeling of excitement swelled, a living, breathing flame that wormed through him in the way it had done a thousand times before.

Life was not cheap, but neither was it certain. Lady Addington had thrown her dice into the corner of honesty, but that did not mean she was trustworthy. Cunning had its own edicts and sometimes surprise was as effective a weapon as force.

She knew the ancient gold marks of Paris. That in itself was revealing. He wondered if she understood the responsibility that accompanied such knowledge, the appreciation of purity, the fight against counterfeit.

His thoughts wandered to the ornament that by pure good chance had come into the Ministry of War's hands, the one he had told Shay of with its accompanying warning.

When the metal had been examined by the *ministère*, those checking its properties had been shocked by the measure of greed inherent in it. The bulk of the ornament was silver, a small slither of gold on the outside, cased with lead at the base to compensate for the weight. A further note attached with a dab of glue outlined what was known of the French connection and their cause, but said nothing of the English receivers.

Whoever had sent it had held an expertise in the properties of the precious metals and when he'd gone to the boarding house in Brompton Place the man who had shot him had whispered six words before he had pulled the trigger.

She sent me to kill you.

Violet? He hoped not, but the small and important clues were beginning to mount.

Sometimes intelligence was simply a matter of waiting for the right place and for the right circumstance. This time, however, he had an inkling that waiting would only be more dangerous. To him?

He shook his head and tried not to breathe in the quiet scent of violets. He wasn't worried about himself—after all, he had been in this game for years. No, it was Lady Addington who was in trouble, he was sure of it, whether it was of her own making or someone else's. Lifting the ring from its bed of paper, he put it back on the third finger of his right hand. He had not missed it, which was surprising, and more surprising still was the fact that he had wanted her to have it, to wear it, a part of him with her, the fiery-headed widow of a man who was had died in an unfortunate accident.

Violet Addington held secrets in her eyes, but he liked talking to her. He liked watching her. He liked the smattering of freckles across her nose and the way she used her hands when she spoke. She made him laugh and her light settled his isolation.

He'd seen her at the Creightons' ball before she had noticed him. She was gracious and charming, but there was something held back. She'd been rattled when she had known he was there and no doubt the woman she had been talking to had pointed out all the ways he was dangerous.

They did that here far more so than in Paris. He could feel the tension in the mamas when he walked by them, protecting their chicks from perceived harm while balancing the attractions of his wealth and title.

Violet Addington observed him in a different way. There was a decided sensual slide underneath the mask of cordiality.

She was no untried girl, no ingénue who would demand careful handling and slow measured steps. She was no longer young and that attracted him, too. He wanted her in his bed underneath him, her tresses of fire falling across white sheets and staining their tryst with passion.

He wanted her as he had never wanted a woman before and that was saying something, for he'd seldom been short of female companionship.

Reaching down, he adjusted the fit of his breeches as they tightened around an arousal that was growing with each passing thought.

God. She might be the poisoned chalice he had been sent to expose. His French *ministère* wanted the matter settled, but someone else here did, too, and the cache of gold that had been hidden away had not materialised at all.

A wind outside battered the thinness of glass and brought the spiky branches of a chestnut close against the southern wall of the town house. It was freezing and he was sick of the aching cold of the climate. His head still hurt where the miscreant had got in that one lucky strike and an ache in the arm that he had broken two years ago left him irritable and restless. The dull throb in his side underscored every other pain.

It was long past time to retire from the business of intelligence. He deserved it, damn it, deserved quiet after chaos and mayhem.

But he needed first to see that Lady Addington stayed safe.

Chapter Four

Violet stepped into the jewellery shop in Regent Street with a sense of trepidation and when the door closed behind her, her fingers wound around the blade that she kept in her pocket.

Just in case.

Her motto for the last years of her marriage turned around in her head. Just in case he hits me again. Just in case I have to escape.

She had come to ask the jeweller, Mr Whitely, to release two sets of Addington family jewellery that Harland had sent in to be valued just before he had died. She had found the docket a few months ago in a drawer at the Chelsea town house, but hadn't mustered up the courage to confront Mr Whitely directly. However, with her own source of income dwindling, to say the least, the realised funds from the heirlooms was more than necessary.

Whitely met her as she opened up the front door of his shop and the same dislike she had always felt for the man resurfaced as strongly as it had each time she met him. Lifting her chin, she met his eyes directly.

'Lady Addington.' He said the words a little too breathlessly and she knew that something was not quite right. 'I am unable to see you right now. I wonder if I might call on you instead in the late afternoon, say at four thirty at your town house?'

There was a sheen of sweat on his upper lip and the pulse at his throat was fast. She was so good now at determining the inner workings of others that the thought almost made her smile. But not quite. She did not want this man visiting. She did not wish to entertain even one of Harland's associates now that she did not have to.

'No, I am afraid I shall be busy then, Mr Whitely.' She made it a point to look at the large face of a clock behind the desk.

But then another door opened to one side and a man walked towards them. It was only as the gloom of the alcove was replaced by the light that she understood exactly who he was.

Mr Whitely smiled and tried to put the newcomer at ease. 'If you could just wait for a moment, sir, I shall not be long.'

'Oh, take as much time as you need. I am in no hurry at all.'

The drawn-out tones of an American accent fell easily over the voice of Aurelian de la Tomber. With a heavy brown wig and moustache, he looked nothing like the dashing French Comte who had ladies from nineteen to ninety in thrall.

But it was not just the clothes and hair. He walked more heavily and the tick in one eye was inspired.

What could he be doing here of all places and in disguise? Even as she thought it the worm of a horror began to build. This was more than coincidence, much more.

Left with them both facing each other, Mr Whitely had no other recourse but to introduce them.

'Lady Addington, this is Mr Daniel Bernard, newly arrived from the Americas.'

'My pleasure, ma'am,' he said, the amber behind thick spectacles darkening. 'I could not help but overhear Mr Whitely say that he was occupied. If it is my business that holds you up, Mr Whitely, I can easily meet you another time.'

'Oh. I should not wish you to do that, sir,' Violet interjected, this day turning out so strangely that all she wanted was to be home. 'After all, you have come a very long way. Which part of the Americas are you from?'

She saw the muscle in his jaw jump and the quick pucker of a dimple in his cheek.

'New York.' This lie was given boldly. He did not flinch from her gaze. 'Are you also a collector of beautiful things, Lady Addington?'

Straightening herself so that she was not quite so small, she simply smiled. She would tell him nothing else for she had the thought that he was one who could deduce the truth from only a small amount of fact.

'Her husband, Lord Addington, was the collector, but he was killed in an accident.' Mr Whitely now joined the conversation and Violet wished he might not have. 'Unfortunately a horse got loose in the Viscount's stables and clipped his temple in panic. He had no chance, poor man.'

Fumbling with a handkerchief taken from her pocket, Violet dabbed at her eyes. She had found an outpouring of emotion a most effective way to silence others in their desire to speak to her about Harland. Mr Whitely looked taken aback, but she did wonder if she appeared quite upset enough for there was a gleam in the Comte's eyes that held a great deal of question.

'I give you sincere condolences, my lady.' Whitely was now all solicitous apology. 'Mr Bernard was just asking me about the marks on gold. He holds a great interest in the subject, it seems.'

'I am especially keen on the jewellery and ornaments fashioned by Mr George Taylor.'

Violet suddenly wanted nothing more than to escape and she saw that the sweat on Whitely's upper lip and forehead was beading into noticeable droplets. Could Aurelian de la Tomber understand the danger such a statement placed them all in or was he a part of the deception, too?

'You collect his work?' Her voice sounded small and weak.

'Not yet, but I have seen a statue that I am most taken by.'

Shock kept her still, the undercurrents stronger than ever. He spoke of the Taylor statue in her salon, she knew he did, for he had asked her about it once before. She had wanted to remove it, but felt shackled by its history, the small harbinger of warning a reminder of all that she would never do again.

'I see.'

And she did. Saw it all in every colour of dread. Saw how all the lies had come to this point and how there could no longer be any chance of going back.

'I think I shall leave.'

'Might I trouble you for a short lift, Lady Addington? I am feeling faint and probably need to be at my lodgings which are only a few streets away.' She could hardly refuse de Beaumont without causing question.

Once outside and the door shut firmly behind them, the French Comte lost all pretence.

'You should not have come here, Violet.' None of the American drawl remained and his hand on her arm was like a vice. 'It was foolish.'

She noticed that the gold Parisian ring was back on his finger even as she pulled away. 'Let me go this instant, sir, or I shall scream.'

He did just that, but the fury in his eyes was unhidden. 'Why are you here?'

'I imagine for the same reason you are, my lord. To do business with the jeweller.'

He turned at this and began on a different topic altogether. 'I have heard it said that you have an expert knowledge on the values inherent in gold?'

They were in the carriage now and the door was closed behind them.

'My father was a successful jeweller. I grew up with the knowing.' She looked at him full on, the very threads of her existence hanging in a balance. He was French and everything she knew of him was shrouded in shadows. Shifting. Changing. A chameleon. A man of violence. The disguised American. She was heartened by the frown on his face and pushed on.

'I am here, too, because most women enjoy the thought of jewellery, sir, and I am no different.'

The idea of appearing so very shallow stung a little, but it was much better than the alternative.

'Yet I have never seen you wear even a single piece of adornment, Lady Addington. There are things about you that do not quite make sense.'

'I could throw the same accusation at you, Comte de Beaumont. If I had alerted the Home Office of your injuries on the night I found you on Brompton Place, would they have been interested in your movements, do you think? Would they still be now?'

'Are you blackmailing me?'

'I liken it to playing chess, my lord. One move can be checked by another. If you insist on asking questions about me and my family, then you leave me with no other option.'

He leaned forward at that. 'You think it a game, Violet? A small entertainment? What if I told you I believe your husband was murdered?' His head tilted slightly as she gave no answer and he swore. 'But you knew that already, did you not? Then know also that you could be the next in their sights, the wife of a man who was not quite as he seemed. What if I also told you that George Taylor, the jeweller, is dead, too. His body was found in a ditch outside Chichester three days ago and his injuries were substantial.'

Horror consumed her.

'Whatever your husband got involved in was brutal, Violet, and cruel, so if by any chance Addington's gains were also your own I would leave London and disappear immediately.'

'Gains?' She could barely speak.

'When one melts down gold and replaces the bulk of it with silver and lead there is great propensity for a lucrative exchange, but there is also a greater chance of dying for it.'

She lifted her hand and banged hard against the wall of the carriage, glad when it came to a standstill.

'I do not know what it is you speak of, but this is your stop, sir.'

He nodded. She could see the muscles in his jaw moving, though he himself made no effort at all to climb out.

'If you ever have a need for help, Lady Addington, day or night…'

She tipped her head and looked away.

'I shan't.'

He looked at her in a way that broke her heart and as the door shut behind him she watched him move off into the showery rain, the greyness of the city swallowing him up.

The jeweller Whitely was a part of the ring of silence regarding the gold, as was the murdered Harland Addington.

Aurelian had found reference to them both in a letter that he'd come across in the armoire of George Taylor when he had broken into his London premises. In the letter the amounts of gold leached from the largesse sent from France was set out in plain black and white.

He had only found the sheet of paper because it had fallen down the back of one of the drawers in the desk. A fact which attested to the care those involved had taken in leaving no trail of their activities whatsoever.

The question now was had Violet Addington known either about the gold coming in from France or the hidden thievery of her husband? What could have been gained in such an endeavour, for surely it was only a matter of time before the ruse was discovered. He wondered how many ornaments had been made even as Harland Addington's gambling addiction came to mind.

From what he had discerned, nothing had ever been put in place to stir up the hornets' nest of resistance in Britain that had been promised and paid for. It had been pure greed that had motivated those here receiving the gold right from the start.

Nothing quite added up, though, for neither Whitely nor Violet Addington had left London in the past week. So had George Taylor been killed by another?

Was the string of murders a culling of people who knew the pathway of the French gold perhaps? Until there was only one left to claim it in silence and without recrimination?

Where did Lady Addington sit on such a ladder?

He swore softly and hailed a hackney cab that happened to be passing. Once home he would write down the patterns and find the thread. It was only a matter of time before it would form into the truth.

* * *

Violet stood in her room that night and went over every second, every word, every inference of her meeting with Aurelian de la Tomber. A lump rose in her throat and she swallowed it back, gritting her teeth against such weakness.

Desolation was always just a heartbeat away, the loss of self and life and love. How often had she stood on the edge of a precipice looking down, a long way down, the crumbling edge of the cliff under each foot. Closing her eyes, she could feel herself falling and opened them up again quickly.

She did not know which way to turn. George Taylor was dead and she had seen that the jeweller Whitely had known of it, too. Who would be next?

Aurelian de la Tomber was here to recover the French gold, for there were shadows of knowledge in his amber eyes and his words about the gold content in the statue sent to France were telling. Was he one of the senders or was he someone far more menacing?

Where did he stay here in London? How could she find out without raising suspicion? When she had sent back his ring she had left it to her butler to find the address. She could not now ask him of it without inciting question.

De Beaumont had warned her in the carriage today with a fierce and honest anger. *You should not have come here. It was foolish.*

But he did not know the half of it and she would never tell him. To protect herself she needed to maintain an innocence.

Grimacing, she knew that was also a lie. She was not an innocent. Not by a very long shot.

Her sister-in-law Amaryllis had gone to bed with a headache tonight and her two children looked haggard and drawn after returning from a small holiday with their aunt in Bath. Michael and Simon worried for their mother and at ten and thirteen she could see their sense of uncertainty and sadness.

Pray to God her sister-in-law remained strong enough to cope. If she did not, then all this would be so much more difficult.

Amara was falling apart before Violet's very eyes, duplicity leaking out in ill health. Well, Harland would not ruin what was left of his family, Violet decided, as she crossed to the armoire in the alcove and removed a small key from its bed of green baize.

Folding out a corner of her rug, she pushed down on a loose section of timber and then lifted up an ornate wooden chest in the space between and inserted the key.

The copy of her note written to the French Embassy when she had sent the statue was there on top, standing as a protection for her part in trying to end the duplicity if she needed it in the end. Harland's threat of killing her lay folded in ribbon, as well, his black writing clearly indicating his anger. She did not even glance at this, but dug deeper.

Here. The necklace was wrapped in tissue and when she opened it the broken gold and sapphire circle spilled out. Her fingers gripped it and pressed down, the jagged gold hurting her skin. She had found this on the floor of Harland's study at Addington after a small group of people had come up unexpectedly to see him. There had been an argument and they had left with the slam of doors and a distinctly heard threat of dying for the gold.

These would be the clues that de Beaumont must be trying to find. All the ruin and lies and the pointers as to whom was involved.

She heard Amaryllis cough in the adjoining chamber, her malady from the autumn still hanging on with a fervour. She heard the bells, too, ringing out midnight over a sleeping London town.

'You will not win, I swear it,' she whispered and hated the anger that was building inside her. It was to Harland she spoke and to his soul lost in the depths of the hell he had put them all through.

She needed to see that no one would come after them. She also needed to understand just exactly who Aurelian de la Tomber, Comte de Beaumont, really was.

Then she would make her next move.

She met the French Count three days later at a small soirée her godfather, Charles Mountford, had invited her to. She saw Aurelian de la Tomber the moment she arrived, standing on the other side of the room, head and shoulders above every other man present. She was pleased she had worn her ugly cap and a gown that covered every bit of her.

'I have been wondering how you fared, my dear.' Charles smiled at her in the way he always did, a sort of wistful memory of her mother present.

'London suits me and I am happy here, Uncle Charles.'

'It is good to see you have shed the widow weeds. Colour brings out all the parts of you that were in the shade before.'

'It is time for me to move on, I think, time to find some other purpose for myself in life and focus on the future.'

'Have I not always told you that, my dear? Your mother will be smiling from up above to hear of such a decision. But now come, I want you to meet the Comte de Beaumont, newly returned from Paris. He is an interesting man.'

Gritting her teeth, she followed Charles with a good deal of hesitation. As the Comte looked up at them some primal interest showed before he could school his face.

'This is my goddaughter, Lady Addington, Comte de Beaumont, a girl of good name and sense.'

'We have met' came the rejoinder. 'At the Creightons' ball a week or so back.'

'Indeed.'

Her godfather gave the impression that he had known already of their first introduction and Violet wondered why he should have tested them.

'In that case I shall leave you both to become reacquainted and see to my other guests.'

Within a few seconds he was gone, winding his way to the far side of the room. Charles was up to something, Violet thought, but the Comte's first words chased such ruminations away.

'I see you have not taken my advice, Lady Addington.'

'Advice?'

'To leave London. To go to safety.'

He spoke quietly so that his voice did not carry and she did the same.

'I want neither trouble nor any added attention, Comte de Beaumont, but…'

'I think it is already too late for that.'

'I don't understand?'

'How close are you to Mountford?'

'He was a good friend of my late mother and he is my godfather.'

He had taken her arm now and walked with her out on to an enclosed balcony where no one else had as yet come to stand.

'Your husband gambled. Large amounts, it is said, too large for the income he was receiving.'

'Not every marriage is an easy one, my lord.'

She could barely believe she had admitted that, she, who was so private about her own affairs. The words seemed to have taken him aback for he looked concerned, his golden eyes full of it.

'Do you have other family?'

'A sister-in-law, my lord.'

'Who do you talk to, then, confide in?'

The silence between them was telling.

'It is said that Harland Addington's sister Amaryllis Hamilton has been seeing a doctor for a melancholy of spirt.'

The words made her freeze. He knew. She knew he did. Knew all about her and Amara and Harland.

Was he a spy? She had it on good account that Summerley Shayborne was a friend of his and Viscount Luxford had been Wellesley's first officer of intelligence.

A French intelligence officer, then, sifting through truth and lies? It suddenly all made sense.

George Taylor was in the mix, too, as was the jeweller Whitely. So many moving parts indicating what might have happened and, if someone should combine those pieces to the bits that she knew...

She felt her world shift and re-form, the danger close and dreadful. When Douglas Cummings ambled across to join them she stiffened.

'You look like a flower in full bloom on this cold and wintry evening, Lady Addington.'

Chancing a look at Aurelian de la Tomber, she perceived astonishment in his eyes. The French were known for their gallant courtly manners, but the Comte did not seem to be at all of that bent. If anything, he observed Cummings in the way a hunter might have eyed a deer in some woods. Ready to pounce. In for the kill.

A new question. Was anything ever just simple with the man?

'Perhaps you might take a turn around the room with me, Lady Addington?' Cummings reached for her arm and tucked it into the crook of his.

At the first steps she felt a sense of loss that took her breath away. She wanted to be closer to Aurelian de la

Tomber. She wanted to stand beside him and be sheltered by his strength. That thought had her breathing in deeply. Warmer than warm, if she were to be honest. Hot and wanting. The French Count effortlessly made her feel things inside that she never had before.

What was happening to her? What part of such an admission made any sense at all? She concentrated on what Cummings was now saying.

'Come to the Vauxhall Gardens this Saturday, my dear. Bring your sister-in-law, too. The band this week is a particularly good one and I know you would both enjoy it.'

Violet was astonished at his invitation and uneasy about it.

'I shall check my appointments. I am not quite sure of what was planned this weekend and my sister-in-law keeps her own social calendar.'

'Were they close? Your husband and Mrs Hamilton?'

'Not particularly. I think after the loss of her own husband she drew inward.'

'Yet you have flourished. I have noticed the differences in you lately.'

A further confidence she wished he had not made at all.

As she passed by Aurelian de la Tomber and her godfather again she saw how they both watched her. There were things afoot here that she could not understand, undercurrents and vibrations. Charles Mountford had always been like a favoured uncle, but today even he held an expression that was not familiar.

She had come out of mourning only a few weeks ago and maybe it was this fact that accounted for Cummings's sudden want for more of their acquaintance. She knew that black had never truly suited her so that the bright colours she now favoured were like the shedding of a chrysalis she'd been trapped in for too long even despite the fact that all her gowns were old. But Charles Mountford's expression showed a good amount of worry as well as anger, emotions replicated on the face of de la Tomber next to him.

Perhaps they were working together? This thought was as surprising as it was hopeful.

She wanted Aurelian to be an honest man. She wanted him to be good and true and moral in the way Harland had never been. She wanted to make love to him in the moonlight and feel him inside her.

Her heart began to race. She had always been so very unexcited about sexual intimacy. It was one of the things Harland had hated about her the most.

Yet here she was imagining the Comte above her, his arms tightening as he leaned down to take her mouth.

'Would you like me to find you a drink?' Douglas Cummings leaned in closely. He had been eating onions, she thought, the sour smell of them strong. When she nodded he departed immediately, leaving Aurelian in his stead.

'Can I visit you tonight, Violet?'

Her heart thumped loudly in her ears.

'Yes.'

When she turned to look again he was not there.

Had he truly just said that or was it some strange trick in her mind? Exhilaration was an emotion she had not had much practice in after her dreary years with Harland. She felt a small trickle of sweat run between her breasts.

Charles had come across again, too, and his smile was strained.

'Perhaps you should consider taking a holiday, my dear, to a place of warmth and beauty. The grandeur of Rome comes to mind with all its antiquities and history.'

Another man with good advice. She made herself smile. 'Perhaps I shall do that.'

'I will write a list of all the places that cannot be missed,' he continued, a tone in his voice that could be construed as relief. 'Travel always broadens the mind and stretches one's boundaries of knowledge.'

'Did you hear that the jeweller George Taylor had died in Chichester?'

A frown crossed his forehead. 'I have said before it is better for a lady to let such affairs be dealt with by men who understand these things.'

'You did give me that advice,' she responded and finished the pale, tasteless orgeat punch she had been offered on arrival. 'And while it is kindly meant, I find myself quite up to the task of sorting out my own affairs these days.'

'A mistake, my dear.'

'For whom, Uncle Charles?' She would not back down. This was exactly the sort of game that Harland had played with her.

'You have no idea of the people you would be up against should you delve into your late husband's past.' His eyes found de Beaumont talking with another man over by the generous doors.

'People like the Comte?'

'He is a man whose reputation is unequalled.'

'In society? As a hero or a villain?'

Charles lifted his own glass to his lips and drank deeply. 'My advice to you, Violet, would be to find another husband and concentrate on being a wife. This is the avenue that could bring about your true happiness. I am certain your mother would have furnished the very same advice.'

Violet made herself smile prettily as she turned to the room, her heart racing under the pretence. Charles had his fingers in many pies and she had known that he had watched Harland closely. The Home Office, which he headed, was, after all, the ministry designed to keep England safe from any outsiders who might try to harm it.

'You have changed something in here, I think. The colour of the walls, perhaps?'

'Yes. It was blue, but my wife insisted upon a shade of yellow.' She could see he was relieved by the new topic.

And so the conversation rolled into the dressing of the home's interiors and to the antics of his son who had just started at university that very year. Safe discussions and far from the true intent of those others. As she talked she searched for the enigmatic Comte de Beaumont, but she could no longer see him anywhere.

* * *

Amaryllis had finally retired, her sister-in-law staying up far later tonight than she had in months. Bidding her farewell, Violet made her own way up to bed, asking a servant to douse the lights below as she went. Did the Comte watch on from somewhere close? Would he even come? Upstairs she left two candles alight and dismissed her lady's maid.

'Go and find your own rest, Edith. I shall see you in the morning.'

'Thank you, my lady.'

The girl was off before other duties might come her way and Violet locked the door behind her.

Last time Aurelian de la Tomber had come from the balcony. This time, no doubt, he would do the same. She stripped away her shawl and laid the dark green velvet fabric across a chair. She no longer felt cold. The heat in her burned like a fire consumed in flame.

She knew the moment he arrived, the air around congealing in anticipation. Tonight he was dressed fully in black, enmeshed in shadow and night.

'I think Douglas Cummings is a dangerous man.' Not the words she had hoped for. Was it for politics he had come?

She frowned. 'He holds the appearance of one who could hardly swat a fly.'

'Looks can be deceiving.'

'Like yours were at the jeweller's?'

He ignored that and carried on. 'Cummings works for Charles Mountford and has access to all the documents that come into the Home Office.'

He was serious. It was not a personal dislike, but something much more sinister.

'Did you ever see him at Addington Manor? When your husband was alive?'

'No. But he was the sort that Harland enjoyed most—a man of subservience and gratuitous compliments.'

Crossing the room, she poured each of them a drink. The cognac was from Charente and the best that money could buy. This could not go on, these half-truths they were telling each other, for she felt that she was simply standing on air. Squaring her shoulders, she turned.

'Who are you, Comte de Beaumont, and why are you asking such questions of me?'

'Why do you think I am here?' He was so good at turning the question back on the one who had asked it.

'I think that you are investigating my husband.'

There, it was said, out in the open where she could not take it back.

'Everything I hear about Harland Addington makes me dislike him.'

She took a good sip of the brandy.

'There were a few good parts.'

'Such as?'

'He spent much of the year away from our estate.'

'So absence did not make the heart grow fonder?'

She ignored that and posed her own query. 'Who do you work for?'

'The Ministère de la Guerre in Paris.'

An unexpected honesty. She'd heard of them, of

course, the shadowy and powerful arm of Napoleon's policing of the city. No small and insignificant group. The shock of it held her still.

'Your husband is accused of stealing gold sent to him from France for purposes he failed to deliver on. I found a document a few days ago saying as much with his name and yours upon it.'

The words fell like sharpened swords on any hope that he represented a neutral ground or that it was for some other misdemeanour her husband was being followed. 'I do not know what you speak of. I never signed any such agreement.'

And there it was again, that trust. She told him things she had never allowed another to know before. It was astonishing.

'If this blows up publicly, you will be implicated.'

I am already, she almost said, almost blurted it out here in the silence and with the cold of the winter licking at the night. But it was not just her story to tell and there was danger for anyone whose identity was exposed. How well she understood that.

Aurelian de la Tomber filled the room as he stood before her, huge and beautiful and overwhelming. He looked as if he was planning to go. She saw him glance towards the door, measuring the passage of space and poised to leave her.

Reaching out, she laid one hand across his arm, feeling the strength in muscle and sinew. For so very long she had been careful, anonymous. For all the years of her adult life she had barely made one decision that only affected herself and her happiness.

'I am sorry for the lies between us, but I cannot make it different.'

His eyes caught in the firelight.

'Cannot because you are a part of it or will not because you are protecting somebody else?'

The truth of that observation seared into the heart of her own connections. He was undeniably clever and he told her the way of it without any apology to her sensitivities.

A dangerous man, then. A beautiful one, as well. A man who inhabited her dreams.

'Say you do not want me here, Violet, and I will leave this second.'

She opened her mouth to speak, but couldn't, for the words of denial stuck in her throat. Then she was in his arms, his mouth claiming hers hard. An elemental taking, his tongue probing deep, one hand winding into the bright of her hair. She tipped back her head and opened further, the melting of her resistance simply taking her breath away.

Harland had never kissed her like this. He had never possessed her. This was not a pretty, quiet kiss or an ordered one. No, Aurelian de la Tomber took, greedily and completely, twisting her so that he could come in further, owning the right of it, stamping his need.

She became a part of him and he of her, her breasts plastered against his chest, the junction of his knees riding the line of her upper thighs. Hard. Fast. Like a fantasy, but a thousand times more vivid. When he bit her lip she nipped him back and he broke off the kiss.

Close up, his eyes were ringed in yellow and feathered in a dark gold-green. The scar on his chin stood out in a welt. But she felt the truth of him, felt the pull of lust and the answering surge of delight. No, that was too tiny a word, too shallow for all that was happening.

'Trust me, Violet. Trust me and live.'

She could hear the accent of France in his words, a foreignness that was bone deep. She could hear the hope, too.

Darkness was all about them, the night, the moon, the shadows, the silence. She wanted him to strip off her clothes and take her hard here, on the floor without resistance. She wanted him to hurt her with love to make her live again, make her real, make her want and cry and laugh. Her hands reached for the buttons of his shirt and slid inwards, her fingers tweaking at the bud of one nipple.

His breathing was as loud as her own, husky, unrestrained and desperate, the kettle drum of his heartbeat roaring in her ears.

A disturbed rhythm, no constant within it, his sex nestled against her stomach, thrust into awareness. Not tame. Not quiet. Neither biddable nor easy. Masculine. Unashamed. Illicit.

Impossible, too. She could suddenly see it in his eyes as he pulled back, there in the quiet of his truths.

'You are beautiful, Violet, and you deserve so very much more…'

The words were so absurdly old-fashioned she wanted to cry. Another man telling her what she did or did not need. Breaking away, she knotted her hair, wiping the fabric of her sleeve across her mouth to remove the taste of him.

'Perhaps you are right.'

She could not argue, not with the world as she knew it changed and unrecognisable. Not at this moment when the future had been stretched before her in a beautiful and flawless line, but was now broken into small and jagged bits.

She was pleased when he was no longer beside her.

Outside he leaned back against the tree he had climbed down, not trusting himself to go any further.

He felt dislocated and empty.

Violet Addington had taken some part of his essence that he could not regather, left there in her room among his passion and lust and need.

The only way he could protect her was by staying away and here he was like a rutting stag in season, a man panting like a green boy to simply climb back up to her chamber and claim what she had offered.

'Hell.'

No one who knew him would have recognised him in that room, a man who had always held full control of his emotions, a man whose secrets were so far buried he could barely remember them himself. And there he had been spilling everything, figuratively as well as almost literally.

He swore again beneath his breath and moved towards the road, careful to stay within the boundary of the winter shrubs and the fence line. If Shay had been in London he would have gone to see him, but his friend had returned to Sussex.

He'd go home to his town house and think. It was past time to crack this ridiculous farce of the missing gold wide open.

Cummings was involved, he was sure of it, and Mountford was trying to keep a lid on every new discovery because the Government both here and in France did not want this scandal to be played out in the public sphere.

Napoleon was interred on Elba and the tides of war were turning towards other things, the hope of diplomacy being one.

Aurelian was happy with that, for the clandestine world of intelligence held its own safeguards. He just wondered why Violet kept slipping into the middle of it with such alarming regularity.

Pray to God it was because of her husband's involvement and not her own, but something was telling him that she was in it much deeper than she let on.

She stood in the place he had left her, listening for the last small noise of his going. She made herself wait even when she could no longer hear him, reaching out in memory, feeling things she had been so very long without.

The memory of Harland's death dropped into the middle of her stillness, how her husband's face had contorted with rage as he died at her feet, the blood running down the side of his temple and into the blonde wispiness of his hair.

She had led the stallion into the stall as soon as Harland ceased to breathe and left the horse there with the body, taking the bloody hammer in her full and voluminous skirts with shaking fingers.

Nothing was ever as it seemed. A lesson she had learned over and over and over again.

Harland's death. The lost gold. Aurelian de la Tomber's appearance in the middle of a road on a sleet-filled night.

Connections linked them, joined them, wound them into each other like skeins of wool, knitted together by expedience and sorrow. And politics.

What was it she had missed in all of this, what final quiet and tiny clue lay there for her to use wisely? She was so good at puzzles, at finding the missing pieces. Even Harland had admitted that.

Shaking her head, she dismissed him, a man of foolish greed and threadbare hopes. She thought she had dismantled the potency of the French gold by sending a letter and the ornament to the embassy in Paris, Harland's greed knowing only the bounds that others might place upon him.

But she had not counted on those who surrounded her husband, the sycophants and the lie spinners. She had not taken their deceit into consideration and she should have.

That had been her mistake and it was one that she would not make again.

Trust no one, not even a man who fired her blood and set her heart racing. Perhaps least of all him.

Chapter Five

The note came the next morning just as Violet was about to leave the house with her sister-in-law for a stroll in Hyde Park. After reading the short message she tucked it firmly into her reticule.

She felt sick. She felt scared. She felt as if a terrible truth had finally escaped its tether and was now loose in the world to do as it willed with her. With them. With Amaryllis and her boys, their two lost faces raised up towards her.

There is no future for us now.

Had she just said this aloud? No. Amara still smiled and her maid handed over a warm woollen cloak without hesitation. An old cloak of violent green with a vibrant multicoloured brooch pinned near the collar.

Shockingly obvious. The overt and delicious taste of flaunting rules she'd felt just half an hour ago when choosing the garment now felt bitter in her mouth.

It was a target she had just painted upon her person. Hit me. Aim here. Do your best to wipe me off the face of the earth and any other person around me.

Yet she could not exchange her cloak without having to explain such an action. Her taste in clothing had magnified exponentially since throwing off the black of mourning and Amara had challenged Violet on it on a number of occasions. Not in the mean way her brother would have, but in the way of a friend who was trying to protect her against the gossip of criticism.

Her hair this morning was pulled up beneath a purple hat, the plumes of some vibrant country bird streaming from the crown.

Another poor choice?

A further mistake.

Revenge is certain and you will be the next to die.

She felt the weight of the hammer in her hands even though the instrument of death had long since been disposed of. Well, she would not waver. Women were the steel and the steering rod of a family and if she had forgotten this once with Harland's bullying then she would never do so again.

It was up to her to make sure that what was left of her family stayed safe and she was damned if anyone would hurt them again. Fury beat in her temples and anger sent her blood in fast and ever-widening circles.

'You look flushed, Violet. I hope you are not sickening for the same malady of the chest that I was afflicted with?'

'I am certain I am not, but perhaps we should leave the walk till tomorrow?'

'If you feel unwell, my dear, then you must, but I

will take a quick stroll to get the boys out for a few moments.'

The flame of hope for an easy retreat spluttered and died as Violet regrouped.

'Then I shall accompany you, Amara, for fresh air is supposed to be a tonic for one's health.'

The carriage was outside and waiting, a footman standing at attention near the opened door. Reidy was absent today and the young driver on the box tipped his head as she approached. Everything held peril. The openness of the small green opposite which could harbour a murderer, another conveyance passing down the street, the strangers who walked in this part of the road. It was as though she was open to every jeopardy.

She did have her wits, though, and the small sharp knife in her pocket that she seldom ventured anywhere without.

Michael and Simon were not toddlers, after all, and if there was trouble she could simply shout to them to run and stand the ground herself to make certain that they were safe. A dread began to gather, the cold of early February clinging to her bones, the same feeling she had had with Harland for all those years of being his wife.

Revenge is certain and you will be the next to die.

The note mentioned revenge. Revenge for what? For the gold and her part in breaking open the existence of such a betrayal? For Harland's death or her hatred of everything he stood for? So many pathways of revenge. But why now after all these months should she suddenly feel threatened? What had changed?

The Comte de Beaumont had come into her life and she had known from the first moment of meeting him that he was a man to be reckoned with. Had he sent the note? She could not believe that he might have as there'd been so many private conversations between them to suit the purpose of threat so much better.

The death in Brompton Place had also been a part of all this, she was certain of it. Had the murder there heightened the stakes and pulled the thief from a shadow of silence?

'You are quiet, Violet. I have had an offer from Mr Cummings to accompany him to the Vauxhall Gardens this coming Saturday. His sister and brother-in-law will be in the party. I think I shall accept the kindness.'

Lian's words of warning came to mind and Violet frowned.

'Harland was a close acquaintance, so perhaps I should not go?' Amaryllis continued speaking, her tone uncertain as she took in Violet's countenance.

'I did not know that Mr Cummings and Harland were acquainted. He never came up to Addington Manor.'

'It was in London that I saw him. You did not leave the country much, but I used to go down to the city quite often. It must have been here I was introduced to him.'

Violet closed her eyes, trying to think. She was certain that the initials of one 'D.C.' had been on a list she had found in the locked bottom drawer of Harland's desk just after he had died. Were these men his associates in crime? Did Douglas Cummings have some knowledge of the loss of gold and could he be as dangerous as Aurelian predicted?

My God, today just kept throwing problems her way and now she did not quite know how to tell Amaryllis that she shouldn't go to the Gardens without also having to tell her of some of her suspicions.

If Amara saw the list of initials, she could be in even greater danger than she was now. Ignorance in the face of violent greed was probably the safest stance to maintain.

She cursed the soul of her dead husband yet again for all the problems that he had left them with. A coward. A sycophant. An immoral and arrogant man who saw himself as the very centre of his universe. A man who fancied himself as the key player in the politics of subversion between England and France and yet had taken much of the gold and used it for himself. Her eyes flicked across the faces of her two nephews. They were pale and withdrawn. She did not even know how much they could have seen of the events at the stables when Harland had died, for Amaryllis had always kept them close so she had no true gauge on their involvement. Violet remembered hearing footsteps running by and after Harland's death they had become quieter and less bold. The very thought of what the truth could do to them made her push such a thought away. Children knew very little and yet believed in everything.

She frowned because it had been so very long since she had felt truly whole and hopeful.

'The Minister Mr Charles Mountford has called to see you, my lord.' Aurelian's servant stood straight as he gave the name.

'Send him in, Simpson.'

Lian hoped that the surprise he felt was not reflected on his face. What the hell could Mountford want? He opened the drawer beside him so that his pistol was at hand, glad he kept the weapon primed and ready as a matter of course. Surely the man didn't mean to confront him with force in his own house and in front of a battery of servants? Within a moment Mountford was before him, hat in hand and the steely grey of his hair reflected in the light.

'De la Tomber.' As he walked through into the room he turned to shut the door behind him, a quick flick of the lock alluding to other darker things. Standing still as this was done, he looked around.

'Is it safe here? To talk?'

'Perfectly.'

'I want to relate something to you in complete confidence and strictly between ourselves. I am relying on your honour, you understand? This cannot be allowed to be public information.'

'Then now might be a good time to tell you that I work for the Ministère de la Guerre in Paris. Ah,' he said after a few seconds. 'But I see that you already know that?'

Knowledge lay in Mountford's eyes, revealing a

recognition between those who were immured in the murky depths of intelligence.

Lian continued. 'And my guess is that you think I am involved in the scandal of the missing gold. The gold the supporters of Napoleon Bonaparte sent in order to find a foothold for resistance in England.'

'Well, I have my questions and doubts about you and the presence of the gold is certainly a topic of interest in the Home Office but I am not here today for that. I am here because I think Lady Addington is in jeopardy.'

'Hell.' The tone of the discussion had changed completely.

'And I want to keep her safe.' Mountford's confession sounded genuine and heartfelt. 'She is my goddaughter and I promised her mother I would watch out for her.'

'How is she in danger?'

'She is right at this moment making her way to Hyde Park to have a walk with her sister-in-law and two nephews. An overdue enjoyment of winter sunshine, I should imagine. The small Addington party will arrive in about ten minutes. The thing is, and this is where you come in, I think Violet has been compromised because of some of the unlawful actions of her late husband, Harland Addington. One of my agents reported word on the street that she is the target of those who wish her harm, great harm. I think she has a need for protection from someone who would see those minions as amateurs and deal with them effectively and quietly.'

'And you hope that someone will be me?'

Mountford was implying that he, as the Minister in charge of the Home Office, could not deal with the perpetrators without being tied up in red tape. He was delegating such violence to Lian, a member of a French agency known for its use of violence. There were seldom coincidences in intelligence, a place where survival often harmonised with the need for pragmatism.

From the tone of his words Lian also realised the perpetrators were not from the political arm of either England or France. Mountford wanted the matter dealt with quietly. He did not want a scene, but he also did not want Violet Addington hurt.

This was to be no official mission. Hyde Park would be crowded with the ladies and gentlemen of a society who would be so much better off not seeing the crawling underbelly of violence.

Already Aurelian was moving, reaching for his gun and pocketing it.

'Which gate?'

'Stanhope.'

'Who else do you have there?' He could not believe a man with as much influence as Mountford had would want to be completely cut off from the happenings.

'Douglas Cummings and a few others from the Office. They have orders to watch Violet.'

'Do you trust him? Cummings?'

'Yes, but at the Home Office we must play the cards we are dealt. To show our own in such a public place leaves us vulnerable, you understand.'

'A questionable morality is what you are after, then?'

'As long as it is also mindful of keeping things… private.'

Grabbing the bottle of cognac, Aurelian put it down on the table. 'Stay here for five minutes before leaving.'

Then he was out of the door, calling for his horse to be brought around and hating the way his heart beat so fast he could feel it solidly thick in his throat.

He saw Lytton Staines and Edward Tully the moment he dismounted inside the park, the height of each of them singling them out in the crowd. Tying his horse to a post, he wandered across to them, doing his best to locate Violet.

Where was she? Was he too late already? Had the attack occurred in the first seconds of her being here, a far more professional set-up than Mountford had imagined?

Catching at the watch at his waist, he looked at the time. Three o'clock. A fashionable hour even on a fresh blue winter day with its smattering of sunshine. The promenading, peacocking and flirting was at its height, the aristocrats of London society drawn to Rotten Row as they partook in the complicated and important rituals of elevating themselves above all others in dress, conversation and appearance.

Where the hell was Violet? Lian peered through ankle-length drab coats and the gilded carriages travelling by, through the cloths of velvet and coloured wools and the unimaginable headgear of courtesans. The plainer attire of wives and mothers was prevalent also as was the rush of youths and children.

After a month of rain it was as if the world had suddenly blossomed in the sunshine. There would be above a hundred people here, he guessed. At least it was not the thousands that a summer afternoon in the high Season might have claimed.

He had a quick glimpse of Cummings through the crowd, the pinched face of Mountford's junior fastened upon him. A number of others hung close, the rigid set of their shoulders telling Lian something of the structure of seniority in Cummings's department. Men who would do as they were told. Men with too much to lose should they take a misstep.

No, it was not from this group that the threat would come. Cummings and his men were too out in the open, too obvious. It had to be someone else. Someone unremarkable and blended. He still had not seen Violet, though, and his worry mounted.

The park was busy at this time in the afternoon, full of riders and strolling groups. The winter sun had finally showed itself after weeks of grey coldness and people were making the most of this small strand of calm. It reminded Violet of some Bruegel painting, the camaraderie, the community, a moment caught in time even if the players in this tableau were better dressed and far more wealthy.

She made herself watch the faces and the way people moved. She was pleased when a friend of Amara's came over to join them as her focus on anything untoward could be better applied with her sister-in-law deep in conversation. The boys had gone their own ways, too, melding with a group of other youths over by the Serpentine. She hoped they would stay there, safe.

She saw him at a distance, the Comte de Beaumont, walking with the Earl of Thornton and the Honourable Edward Tully. The three of them had the attention of every lady from one end of the path to the other. Aurelian de la Tomber looked indolent and relaxed, the smile on his face suiting his demeanour. In the sun, the dark of his hair had shades of red and russet and a lighter chestnut brown. She was glad he did not watch her though she was certain that he knew she was there.

Lian swore beneath his breath and stretched his mouth into a smile. Lady Addington looked like some advertisement for the wearing of bright colours in every garment she had on. If there was threat here it would have no trouble at all in finding her. He did not move closer for he wanted to watch the lie of the land.

Did she not realise the danger of it all? He thought perhaps she did for her stance was rigid, her right hand pushed into a pocket. Did she have a weapon? Could she use it? A cloud covered the sun momentarily, dousing the bright of the day into shadow.

A small group of elderly women were walking towards her. Nothing untoward there, he thought, and trawled more widely. There were so many damn trees in the park and even without their summer greenery the trunks were all wide enough to obscure someone.

Cummings was moving back to the gate behind him, signalling his men with him. Perhaps they had seen something? Aurelian's glance took in a group of men at a further distance and a single gentleman walking at a slow pace along a parallel pathway.

'You seem preoccupied, Lian?' Lytton asked this and he made himself smile as he replied.

'It's the first good day in a while and there are many people out.'

'Including the beautiful Addington widow?'

Edward Tully laughed. 'Lady Addington has made it clear to all those who admire her that she has no time for suitors. She wants a quiet life. She told me that herself after I offered to accompany her to a luncheon party a few weeks back.'

Staines stopped in his tracks and frowned. 'She has only just come out of mourning, Ed. She could hardly be seen on your arm given the recent death of her husband.'

'He was a dolt. Nobody ever had any time for him.'

'You knew him well?' Lian looked over at Tully.

'He was in my class at school. He was always very good at putting people down.'

Violet had turned now and was heading off towards the south end of the park, her sister-in-law and another woman ten yards behind her. Why had she done that? Lian wondered, even as the answer came with a rush.

She was frightened. She had seen someone further on. Somebody she did not want to meet. Someone she knew. The hand in her pocket had delved deeper now and her stride had lengthened.

His glance took in the single gentleman who was closer and the elderly women who were now stopped.

Excusing himself, he hurried across the grass, the ground thick with decaying autumn leaves. Not quite running, for such a motion would bring more attention than he welcomed.

Then everything slowed down, the single man crossed at an angle and took Violet's arm to pull her with him, a blade he held at her breast gleaming in the sun, the drops of red that dribbled from her hand as she tried to stop him, the pale of her face and the terror in her eyes. A hat of purple plumes fell from her head, the bright of her hair like a beacon in the sunlight.

Lian gripped the offender and the knife cut deep into his own flesh. Then the weapon fell groundwards, useless underfoot. He kicked it away as his good hand found his own blade.

'Keep walking. Don't make a sound or I will kill you. Do you understand?' Steel found that soft spot in the assailant's back just above one kidney and he pressed closer, heartened by the nod of the offender. Not a scene, then, but a quiet and unnoticed tussle as the world of intelligence operated right under the noses of an unmindful public.

Violet looked shocked.

'Go home, Violet, and stay home. Mountford will see you safely there.'

Already he could see the Minister coming their way, any indolence gone now.

'And y-you?'

He did not answer as he jerked the offender back down the path and out of the way of the group of women who stared at him in horror. The shout of youths further off had them all turning.

'Let him go, you French bastard. He's English and he did not do anything to you.'

As the ruffians closed in, Aurelian stopped and stood his ground. He looked as if he didn't care one way or another about their presence, his face a mask of cold indifference. Violet could see no sign of the knife he held.

'I'd advise you to go home before you are hurt.'

'There's five of us and one of you.' The largest boy puffed out his chest and moved forward.

'Can you walk with a broken leg? Can you see without eyes?'

The group hesitated, not perceiving in the one they were harassing any of the usual fear. Some other thing lay there, too, on Aurelian de la Tomber's face. Recognition of what this all meant, Violet thought, for someone must have tasked them to expose him. The web just kept growing as the spiders got busier.

Lytton Staines and Edward Tully had cut across to stand beside Aurelian and the height and breadth of the three men was more than enough against the younger and smaller foes. With a click of a finger they had departed, scurrying towards a gate to the south, huddled in a tight and angry group.

Aurelian de la Tomber's hand was bleeding badly, but he didn't seem to have even noticed the hurt as he wiped the blood against his breeches. Violet was still shaking from the shock of her assault and an understanding that only a small line had hovered between life and death.

If he had not intervened, she would be dead.

The very fact of her narrow escape made her breathing shallow and her heart race.

Amara was beside her, weeping quietly, her two sons with their wide eyes on Aurelian as he and the others made their way towards the Stanhope Gate.

'My God, Violet. My God.'

Amaryllis seemed stuck on the few words and when Charles Mountford joined them her sister-in-law fell into his arms.

'The man tried to kill Violet. He had a knife.'

'There, there, Mrs Hamilton. The threat is over now and it is better if we do not make a fuss.'

Better, Violet thought. Better for whom? Aurelian had already been exposed and nothing could stop the gossip that must follow.

'Is everything all right, Mr Mountford?' Lady Elizabeth Grainger and her sister sauntered over, their faces alight with curiosity, as were a few others who had stopped to watch Amaryllis crying.

'It is now. Unfortunately the fellow suffers from fainting spells and felt unwell. He is being helped off to his carriage as we speak.' Charles said this in a tone that was entirely believable. A man who still clung to another truth and was trying his best to contain any damage.

'And your hand, my dear?'

When sharp eyes took in the blood at the top of her thumb Violet scraped up resolve and followed

Charles's lead. 'I caught it on my brooch as I tried to aid him and it cut me.'

A simple explanation for complex things.

She was glad when her godfather took over. 'So if you will excuse us, Lady Elizabeth, I shall make sure the Addington party now gets home. A cup of tea is in order, I think.'

'Of course.' Lady Elizabeth smiled, another group of ladies and gentlemen joining her as soon as she had gone ten yards, no doubt wanting gossip. It was how London worked—the unexpected serving as the fodder for dinner tables—and misfortune, in particular, had its own piquant sauce.

In the carriage Amara sobbed softly and Violet reached over to take her hand. 'I am fine. It must have been some sort of a mistake.'

But Violet could see that her sister-in-law knew exactly what had happened and was just waiting for Charles Mountford to be gone. All the horror of Harland's death came back, the lies and the constant fear of danger. She shook her head at Amara's unvoiced concerns and turned to her godfather.

'I think it would be a good thing for my sister-in-law and her two boys to have a holiday away from England for a little while. Italy would be lovely at this time of year.'

This was not said at all as a question and Charles took up the cause just as she knew he would.

'You could all go to Rome for a month and take in the sun and the sights. Good to get away from the cold here. The boys would love the ruins and the…'

Violet let his words run over her as she gazed out the window. Where was Aurelian de la Tomber now? Who was her assailant? She would not leave England herself, but she could see the hope of a time away in the faces of her nephews. Perhaps that would persuade Amaryllis? She prayed it could be so.

Her hand throbbed, but Aurelian's wound had been so much worse than her own. She understood more about him now. He was as dangerous as they came, his movements in the park speaking of elegant force and careful precision. An expert in violence. A man who was used to death.

She had barely understood the way he had so quietly defused the situation until it was over and she was safe. He'd stopped any harm without fanfare or noise, a quick twist of his arm and the man was caught in his grip, the blade clattering uselessly underfoot. She had seen the strain of Aurelian's grasp on her assailant's face, his eyes bulging and the pulse in his neck fast.

She had understood his intent, too, for the Comte de Beaumont was not a man to bandy purpose. If she had not been impressed by such deliberate force, she might have been truly horrified. The dark of his eyes were pools of twin peril, the danger in them magnified by a stillness that was unfathomable. The ruffians who had called out insult had no idea at all whom they dealt with or of what they had just embroiled themselves in.

'I think we should like to go abroad.' Amaryllis's voice interrupted her musings. 'A holiday away from England might allow us the chance to relax. It has been a hard few years, after all.'

'I could book you passages for this time next week if that would be suitable.'

Uncle Charles wanted them away. Quickly.

When they had reached the town house Amara scurried upstairs, but Charles asked if he might have a word. In the library, he looked concerned.

'You are pale, my dear. Is your hand worse than you are saying?'

'No. It is only a scratch. It was a shock, though. What will happen to the man the Comte took away?'

She was tired of pretence.

'He will be interviewed. Perhaps he is simply crazy.'

'How did you know to be there at the park? At this time?'

'We had heard things about a plot of revenge.'

'Revenge?'

'I am sure the vitriol was directed at your late husband. It is just unfortunate that you were involved.'

She nodded and smiled. 'Of course. That can be the only explanation.' The note in her pocket burned into guilt like a hot coal.

Much later, with Violet's hand bandaged and Mountford gone, Amaryllis came to her bedchamber.

'I have seen him before, the man who attacked you. Harland knew him.'

Violet nodded. She had recognised him, too, for she had once met him in London, in Harland's company.

'So it is probable this is not just coincidence, all of

this? Could your assailant know about what happened in the stables?'

Violet shook her head. 'He couldn't.' She infused as much certainty into her words as she was able. 'But I don't think we should take any chances. Italy will be a godsend for you and the children.'

'You would not come?' Shock was in Amaryllis's eyes. 'You would stay behind by yourself? They have tried to get you once and will do so again.'

'I can't disappear for ever and Aurelian de la Tomber will protect me. I know it.'

'Oh, my goodness, Violet. You cannot be serious. All these problems have only happened since we picked the Comte de Beaumont up off the road. The Frenchman is a killer. We saw the blood on him and heard of the murder in the boarding house. He is not a man to trust.'

'We do not know his story, Amara. After today I think we should give him a chance. He was, after all, the one who saved me.'

'Why was he there, then? Have you thought about that?'

'Charles asked for his presence in Hyde Park. He told me so himself for his agents had heard of the threat.'

'The Comte is dangerous, Violet, but I don't think you realise just how much.'

'Good, for I have need of such a one.'

'You cannot mean this.'

'But I do, Amara. For so long we have been afraid. I do not want to be any more. I won't allow it.'

'Being thrown into gaol is a lot worse than being

afraid. We could simply disappear after travelling to Italy and never come back to England.'

'What of your boys? By running away we will consign them to being homeless for ever and without title. For years your brother frightened us, Amara. He took everything that we were and made us…nothing, but I do not have children to protect, there is only myself. That's why you should leave England until all this is resolved. For Michael and for Simon. For their future.'

Amara stood and walked over to the window, pulling back the curtain to look out into the night.

'You are so much braver than me, Violet, and you always have been. I think that is what attracted Harland to you in the first place. My brother held no courage and he knew it. But to choose this? To choose to stay and fight against enemies we have no knowledge of…'

'I will have help. Uncle Charles is an ally.'

'And when these so-called protectors are not with you? You might have learnt how to use a blade well, but could you kill someone if it was necessary? Could you consign your very soul to the hell mine is in already?'

'Yes. For family, I could. For myself I could. Harland left us both fearful with his appalling behaviour and the only thing I truly wish is that he had died earlier, that we had killed him earlier.'

'It was not you, Violet.'

'If you ever say different to the authorities, I will

refute the fact. The boys need their mother and Aurelian de la Tomber will see to it that I am safe.'

'But for me to go and leave you to it?'

'It's what I want and if you are not here I won't be distracted with worry for you all.'

'I don't know…'

Violet knew right then that Amaryllis would do just as she asked.

Chapter Six

He came that evening late, his shadow slipping through moonlight, the white of the bandage on his hand showing in the gloom.

She was sitting waiting for him in her bedchamber, two glasses and a bottle of wine on the table before her.

He was furious.

'You are a liar, Lady Addington, and one who insists on weaving a fable of untruth around yourself and your family. Because of it you nearly died today.'

Aurelian de la Tomber looked nothing at all like the gentleman the whole of society was so enamoured of. No, tonight he looked untamed and savage, the bloodstain on his unchanged clothes a dark brown and the gold in his eyes of glittering fire.

She stood, uncertain as to what to do.

'I am not—'

'Enough.' He stopped her with a wave of his injured hand and his voice sounded hoarse and broken. 'If you think this a game, then you are wrong. George Taylor is dead because of it and you nearly were today.'

'Because of what?' She swallowed as she asked this, but she could not deliver Amaryllis into chaos on a hunch. She had to know what he meant, had to understand the depth of his suspicions. Her heart beat so loud in her throat she thought she might fall, from lack of breath, from shock and from the pure and plain horror of all he accused her of being.

'Where is the gold, Violet? The gold sent from France?'

The sting of his words cut into hope.

'It is gone.'

'Your assailant was certain that you have it.'

'He told you that?'

'He said that you were the one who knew where it went.'

'He is wrong.'

'It seemed to me that he believed it. It is a small strength of mine, this ability to determine honesty, and one that has come in handy on many an occasion. Mountford thinks the man who tried to hurt you in the park was paid well to do so. He is not talking and that is a worry.'

'Why?'

'A professional would demand something, a way of moving forward to suit all parties in question. The closed mouth of this one suggests he is more fearful for his own life than he is about the full wrath of the English law bearing down upon him.'

That truth made her start.

'How did you know him, Violet? You changed your

course when he came into your vision. I got the impression you were afraid of him.'

His eyes slanted against the light and she could hear in his voice a carefully tempered fury. A man at the very end of his tether and showing it.

'I am not your enemy, Lady Addington. It was your husband who was that.'

Her breath shallowed, and the darkness in the room tunnelled into greyness. Sitting down, she took the note from her pocket and laid it down on the table next to her. 'I think he was the one who sent me this.'

'God.' She saw stillness descend as he read it, holding the missive into the light as if the paper itself contained clues. 'When did you receive this?'

'A few moments before I went to the park.'

'Yet you still ventured out?'

'Amaryllis would have gone alone otherwise and I thought…' She could not go on, but he finished the sentence for her.

'You thought he might have hurt her, too?'

'The revenge mentioned is because I killed my husband.' These words fell into the night between them, sharp-edged with meaning.

'Why?'

'He hit me. I hit him back.' She kept it simple, the lie, kept it pared to the minimum.

'Addington was much bigger than you by all accounts.'

'A hammer is unforgiving and he did not expect it.'

More untruth, but he would see the horror of it all on her face, she was sure. What she did not expect was the sadness on his. The price of the life of her family. She would pay it gladly if it meant Amaryllis and the boys stayed safe.

'Perhaps you lie, Lady Addington?'

His words were soft, but the execution made them doubly potent.

'But you cannot know it, truly.' She gave him this without reserve.

'Which leaves us…where?' The gold in his eyes ran molten.

'Right here,' she said and leaned forward, touching the back of his good hand with her fingers, feeling the heat and the competence and the sheer strength of him. 'Here in this room together with all of our secrets and lies. I need protection and I am willing to pay for it.'

His fingers turned and curled over hers, eyes rising to lock on to her own.

'How?'

'I can see that you want me. You would not have come here otherwise.'

He laughed at that. 'You are bold, Violet Addington, but are you also foolish?'

'I am a twenty-seven-year-old widow who is soon to be twenty-eight. It is not permanence I am petitioning you for, *mon comte*. Only safety. If I am to live at all, I need to be close to you.'

'Close?'

'I have not offered my body to any other and there have been many who have asked, even before my husband died.' She could not make it any plainer.

She pulled away her hand and stood.

If she were to do it, the time would be now. If she faltered, she would lose him and she had no other way of saving all that she had built up. The fury in her made her swallow as did the sheer and utter barrage of nerves.

Unlacing the bodice of her gown, she let the wool slip off one shoulder. Her heart beat like a drum, but too much talking was dangerous. She needed a connection and a truth and this was the only way she might be able to find it. If he refused what she offered, there was no other way to save her world.

Hell. She was beautiful in the candlelight, a burnished flame of fire and ivory and silk and shadow. He had never in all his life seen another like her and the breath rushed from him.

She was tendering herself to him for protection after admitting she had killed her husband. He should be running away from all her complications, but he found he could not.

Tears glistened in her eyes, the grey of them mixed with green as she spoke, her words soft.

'If you are going to risk your life for me, Aurelian, like you did today, then I want to give you something in return.'

'As a duty?'

She shook her head.

'As a troth. I am not a virgin. I am not a green girl. There is nothing innocent you could take from me.'

He frowned. Did she not know that lovemaking

was not all about taking? There was giving in it, too, and such things created bindings.

The fury in him had settled a little. She was scared and she was lonely and fright made her pupils larger.

Reaching out, he drew his finger down the line of her breast, softly and with care. The skin all around his touch puckered into goosebumps, the nipple hardening into a tight and small bud as he watched her take in breath. There were things he did not know about her, big things that might change his world. Things like duplicity and greed and treason.

'Harland was disappointed in my…skills…as a bride.'

These words came in a whisper. She made an attempt to say more, but he stopped her with a simple shake of his head.

'And were you disappointed in him?'

He felt his manhood rise up further.

'Yes.'

He could almost see her mind working and detected a quick thought of flight in the bruised eyes.

'But you would still take the risk of it all?'

Shock held her motionless, but he was closer now, her breath on his cheek.

'I would.'

His forefinger lay across her throat and then lifted, to her chin and then her lips, brushing across the fullness, feeling his way.

She was so beautiful she felt unworldly. He who had been with many different women in his life was suddenly as breathless as she was, and as uncertain.

Sense told him to step back, to move away, to run while he still had the chance, but he couldn't.

Her lips came beneath his, softly at first, finding out, and then slanting, the hitch of lust in him pounding against sense.

She allowed him in, opening under his pressure, wide and deep and true, her fingers clutching at his arms so that he could feel her nails even through fabric.

Drunk with want, he bunched the length of her hair in his fist and slid the injured hand behind her back. He could not refuse her, the risk between them both brutal and known. There were always shades of grey in any act of murder. His own existence had at least taught him that.

She felt him lift her as if she weighed nothing and bring her to the bed, felt the softness of the mattress and the way he came down over her, careful and gentle and yet tempered in need.

The candles flickered, lavender wisps of scent displacing the shadows into ghostly things, a ceiling full of movement. Neither light nor dark, but a place in between. His hand came again around her face, tracing a picture, understanding her want as he pushed at the fabric of her gown, exposing her shoulder and breast further. Shock had her rising, but he did not allow it, keeping her still. His hands were unsteady.

'Violet.'

The hoarseness of his voice and the bigness of his body, skin to skin. She could feel his bones and flesh against her own, calling into tune, like a melody, the rhythm of the night inside. The quiet of the room, the fire in the grate. The snow outside in a cold and growing wind, the solid shield of him above.

Safety.

It held a physical presence that was unnerving.

There was not the slightest of doubt that this man with his dangerous eyes was a warrior, hewn in violence in the hidden corners of the world, the firelight silvering his skin and darkening his hair. But the unknown power of him was exhilarating, like a drug taken in the hope of joy. Well, for her the drug was also forgetfulness, the longed-for oblivion of a past that crowded into her memory and made her feel less of a woman.

This is who I am now.

This woman lying, caught between the fear of temptation and failure and between murder and treason. Her hand turned, clutching at his.

The only time was here, this night, this moment after the danger at the park. The urgency of it undid her and made her fragile when all she wanted was to be strong.

'Do not wait. Do it now. Quickly.'

There, she had said it, out loud, given him the permission that he seemed to seek in his hesitation.

He laughed.

'This husband of yours must have been greedy if he would not see to your needs first, my lady.'

'My needs?'

She did not understand what he was saying. Harland

had only taken and left afterwards, never speaking, never tarrying, hurting her sometimes just because he could.

The patience of a lover was a foreign thing, a different knowledge. She wondered if perhaps he did not want her now that she had allowed such a liberty. An easy lay and a history behind her that was impossible. A broken lady.

He could see her fear and he knew the slightness of her. Too thin in so many places. Trembling. The bruises on her arm angered him as did the bandaged cut on the back of her hand. He looked at her directly and forced her to see just what it was that he offered.

Himself.

But it did not seem to help, the skin across her arms rising into goosebumps and her heartbeat climbing. He controlled each aching muscle in the gloom, ramming restraint into the spaces that need drove into frenzy.

'Let me touch you. Let me taste you.'

Her pupils dilated, filling the grey with blackness, nostrils flaring as they scented a damaged choice.

'Yes.' Barely whispered. Questioning, too. How old had she been when she married Harland? Had she only ever had the one disappointing lover, any expectation buried beneath many years of aloneness?

It was not for love Violet offered her body or even for lust, but it felt like both were there on the edge of midnight after a day of almost death.

Time ceased to exist, the moment stretching into for ever as his lips fell across her nipple. Succulent and sweet and dimpling into hardness as his teeth bit down.

For so many years he had survived on the edge of danger, a man of mirrors and smoke. Here he was present in a way he'd never been before, the smell of her, the taste and the sweet warm feel of ivory skin smattered in freckles writhing under his own.

She liked this. She liked his touch.

He lifted the heavy skirt of her gown, exposing more, peeling back layers.

She did not fight him but stilled, their battle held in truce. His good hand walked up the soft skin on her inner thigh and then delved deeper into the heat. He felt the pull of muscle and heard the quiet sob of breath.

Them. Now. If she wanted words he did not quite know how to give them so he stayed silent, flicking her nipple with his tongue and enjoying the way her hand crawled to his nape and held him there. Joined by flesh and by something else, too. By destiny, he was to later think, or by sheer and brutal luck.

The luck that she had found him in the street on a cold winter night needing help and warmth and faith. Then allowed him succour, without question or deceit.

Lady Addington made his skin shiver. He was fully dressed and yet he could never remember a connection like this one. Today when he thought he might lose her and that he might not be quick enough, his heartbeat had faltered and stopped, the blade in the winter sunshine, her eyes closing in acceptance, the shriek of children playing behind the sharp closeness of death.

She was holding things back. For what purpose or reason he could not tell, but he needed to give her the time and space to come to him in honesty.

Not now, though. Now they needed different truths, truths that were not anyone else's save their own.

His hand went to the fall front on his breeches and he undid the buttons, feeling the solid hardness there.

Would she allow it? Was this where the game ended and reality began? He waited and watched.

When she opened her eyes he saw surprise and shock. But he also saw need.

'I want you, Aurelian…'

Her words were whispered soft and she did not quite say his name like anybody else, lengthening the last vowel and shortening the first.

'Now?'

She nodded and he lifted her leg so that he was nestled closer, more able to find home. His eyes did not waver as he fitted himself at her entrance, the sleekness of her satisfying. Then he was inside, sliding into heaven piece by piece, higher and deeper and further and as she watched him he felt his heart hitch again.

Mine.

He nearly said it, but the licence to do so was not there yet, so he whispered her name instead, three times into the night in the hope that it might become true.

She felt him at her centre, the thickness of him and the heat. Pain was a part of it, as well, because it had been so long since she had lain with a man that her body had become tighter, less accommodating.

He said her name over and over and she could hear in the words an echoed ache as he began to move faster. Any noises after that were deep inside, each groan filling her with an all-consuming desire. Her fingernails dug into his back, the shirt lifted so that she could find bareness. There were scars there, the marks of battle torn into skin, ridging muscle with harder lesions.

Not an easy life. As hard as her own, perhaps? She leaned across and found his mouth, opening her own to take him in.

He was beautiful.

Using her tongue, she explored him, his lips, his mouth, his depth. Owning what she wanted and allowing him to know it. There was no pretence in such a thing, the truth of need a raw and vital spark.

She bit down on him as she withdrew. She did not want him to be gentle. She did not want to beg. She wanted to forget and feel and know all that she had imagined in her lonely marital bed for so very many long years. If it was just to be tonight she wanted the fullness of the sensual. She felt like a pod ready to burst into new life, the rains falling upon her dryness.

Opening further, she tipped back her head as his tongue traced a line on the column of her throat. He'd taken her hands, too, threading them together and pulling them above her so that she was captive against the flame. Stretched out. Ready.

And then he moved hard within her. No simple and quiet taking, but a reach into her centre, marking her, burning her, sending the cold quiet woman she had always been into frenzied rapture.

Exactly this. She smiled in a way that held no humour and he saw it.

'Come with me, Violet. Come with me now.'

And she did, the throb of release building in her throat and in her stomach, until it lit her like a torch with unbridled passion.

She was like a flame caught in the stillness, breathless, stiff and pulsating, each small movement leading to a larger one until her whole body convulsed with need, squeezing him tight.

He came himself in her final throes of release, reigniting all that was quietening and making her groan, loud and then louder, her face contorted in shock and wonder.

His seed spilt within her, deep inside. He had never been so careless before and yet here…

Sealing his mouth across hers, he let himself go, an unaccustomed slip in control, a coupling like no other he'd experienced.

Heaven.

'Hell.' He swore because he felt both found and lost. Found in lust and lost in feeling. The cold part of him that had been frozen ever since he could remember loosened its hold, leaving him reeling.

'Are you hurt?'

Her question filtered through the mists of incomprehension and his hand came forward to frame the lines of her face, shaking his head as he watched her.

'I cannot ever remember being less so, Violet, in all of my life.'

The joining between them held, a connection that underscored everything. He felt the wetness of sex on his thighs and smiled. Her petticoats billowed out beside them like white sails on a darkened sea, her long slender legs burnished with firelight. Unmarked. Shapely. Opened to him. Available.

'What does the name Aurelian mean in French?'

'Little golden one,' he replied and smiled. 'Every one of my family is golden haired and small. I hearkened back to some other bloodline, from the northern climes I always thought.'

'You have siblings, then?'

'A sister. She lives here in England.'

'With you?'

'With my two elderly aunts. They are, however, far more wily than one would think them and many have discounted their power and regretted it. Mama is buried in Normandy, but my father still resides in Paris.'

He had rolled on his back now beside her, his good hand finding the wet warmth of her centre. She did not pull away, but watched him, her lips parting as he pressed in, one finger and then two.

He came in further.

'Here?' he whispered and she groaned as the sweet spot he touched vibrated with heat beneath his fingers. 'Or here?'

Her eyes widened as he worked and then she groaned, reaching for him and bending her knees so that her legs fell full apart.

This time he felt her stomach harden, his fingers each playing in tune, no small game, no quiet, easy ending.

He turned her then and lifted her so that he could find what he sought. And then he was in her softly, feeling his way so that she could know the joy of this touch.

She simply unravelled, right there in his hands, her muscles squeezing him with tightness, keeping him close, finding in the magic her way to the stars, a hitch of breath and the slick tang of sweat before collapsing, in heat and in exhaustion and in something else that he understood exactly.

Wonderment.

'How do you know of this, Aurelian? How can I learn?'

Her lips were swollen from his kisses. The skirt she wore was bunched about her waist and the bodice fell to that place, too, the wool and underclothing framing skin of ivory.

Her hair snaked around her waist and lay on the covers in stains of tousled red, silky and thick with auburn, cinnamon and flame.

She looked like a fine courtesan, well used and satisfied. She looked happy.

'Will you teach me how to please you, too?' This came after a moment, her cheeks flushed and her eyes bright with amazement.

'Are you sore?'

'A little.'

'Then now is the time to show you something else entirely.'

* * *

He had tasted her then, taken her with his mouth and tongue, a softer assault, but so very reminiscent of all the others.

Three times within an hour she had felt the burn of an orgasm when for all the years with Harland she had never understood it once.

Tonight she was like a harlot, like a woman who was used wisely and well. She could have lain there for a hundred years and never moved as she sought to feel all that he gave her again and again, there in the bedroom and the night winding down towards dawn.

She did not care. Aurelian de la Tomber was radiant and life-giving, a lover who understood every nuance of her body. She wanted to wallow in the feeling of it. She wanted to take him in her mouth just as he had taken her, without reservation or shyness. She wanted the break of the day to stay away until there was nothing left of them save feeling.

Her muscles contracted again without his touch and he laid his hand palm down across her stomach.

'You are like *mercure*, Violet. Unpredictable and changing rapidly.'

Quicksilver, she thought, translating from the French and liking the word on his tongue, for the compliment in what he said was no small and vapid thing. For six years she had been so careful. For six years she had been frightened.

Aurelian had freed her here tonight. Freed her body by valuing dominion over her own feelings. There was nothing between them that had been forbidden. No limits.

Quicksilver.

The clock at the end of the room struck the hour of three and Aurelian rose to place another log on the fire. Then he poured more wine and brought her over a glass.

Sitting, she leaned against the headboard, making no effort at all to cover herself. Even that felt marvellously wicked for she saw him observe her in all the places no other ever had before.

'Let us drink to the joy of sex, Violet. The elixir of life.'

She took one sip and then another, but wished he might put his glass down and enter her again. She felt the pulsating, thick want as an ache.

His eyes hooded as she moved and he removed what was left of his clothes so that the hard length of him was easily seen, dusky red in the firelight. The bandage on his hand was so very visible. 'Come here.'

She did.

'Sit down upon me.'

The engorged flesh of him came between her legs and then upwards into her. Upwards and upwards until there was nowhere left for it to go, save against the opening of her womb. He placed his hands on her shoulders and filled her to the very hilt. Only him. Only them. Only his flesh and the knowledge that she would remember this one moment for ever. Joined completely. Her head tilted back and he took her there, too, with his mouth, rasping into softness, a new heat joining the other one, so that rapture and ache came together to create a feeling that was dangerous and consuming. Like a small death. She even forgot to breathe.

Slumped against him a moment later, she felt his fingers moving across her back, drawing circles. Shivering, she came closer, fire diluted now into tiredness. She wanted to sleep for ever.

Lifting her, he drew back the blanket, her breasts pressed against his chest before he laid her down, tucking the warmth about her.

'Go to sleep.'

She nodded, all words gone, the stillness of the night like an echo.

She awoke alone and naked the next morning, her ruined gown draped across a chair beside her bed, nothing left of him save the wetness between her legs, the ghost of passion.

Smiling, she stretched, feeling the ache in places she had not before and revelling in the difference.

Could she love Aurelian de la Tomber after knowing him for such a small time? Did she trust herself to even think this? With Harland she had imagined the same within days of meeting him and then paid for such a stupidity for all of the next six years. Perhaps she was cursed?

A shiver coursed through her. Love or lust? Truth or lies?

She did know one thing, though, to the very centre of her core. She knew she wanted Aurelian de la Tomber to be here beside her with his magical hands and body more than she had wanted anything else in her entire life.

But what would he be feeling? She had been wanton and forward and loose. She had offered him her body for safety and had come away from their tryst into a far more precarious position.

Other bindings now tied her to him and she wondered how she would face him when she saw him at the next soirée. Would he acknowledge what had happened? Small tremors of doubt began to fill her certainty.

Would he feel the same as she did, a man with a wealth of experience with women? A jaded and generous lover?

She turned over in her bed and buried her face in the pillow. Could she survive indifference after this, she who had promised herself never again to be involved with anyone? She had told him her inner secrets and lies. She had allowed him knowledge of things that could destroy her. She had showed him the note and trusted in him.

If he played her false…?

No. She would not think that he might.

It was safety she was after while she unravelled the mystery of who was trying to kill her. Surely at least their unusual bargain would extend to keeping the faith in that.

Chapter Seven

When she finally got dressed and went downstairs at lunchtime, Violet was surprised to find Amaryllis gazing out the windows, all the curtains drawn back.

'I think Charles Mountford must have employed guards to stand out at the front of our house. I sent the butler out to enquire about them and he relayed a message that the men would accompany us on any outings we were to make. They are big men, too, Violet. Take a look.'

Three strangers stood before the town house, each well proportioned and serious. She was certain that they would have carried weapons and also certain that any orders given to them would be well and properly obeyed.

The plot had thickened, then, and Charles obviously did not suspect that the man arrested yesterday in the park was working alone and neither did Aurelian. He had implied that the one who had paid to have her killed was a powerful foe.

Any thoughts of the delights of the night past were

suddenly overtaken with the dread of what might come next.

They were now, Violet thought, essentially prisoners in their own home. Swallowing away alarm, she turned to Amaryllis.

'Have you had any further thoughts about going on holiday to Rome?'

'I have. This morning I sent word to Charles Mountford to ask for passages for myself and the boys to Italy. I wish you would come but…well…' She blushed then, giving Violet a good idea of what she was alluding to even before she spoke. 'The French Comte was here last night? With you?'

She should have known that nothing could be kept a secret. 'He was. I asked him to help provide safety.'

'My maid implied that there might have been more to it than simply that, Violet?'

'I made love with him, Amara, and I do not regret it one little bit.'

Her sister-in-law's hands went to her mouth, the shock in her eyes almost comical.

'What if you become pregnant?'

'I am barren. Surely you heard Harland say that often enough?'

'Perhaps it was a problem related only to my brother?'

'No. He had two children out of wedlock with his favourite mistress in London. He held their portraits in his pocket and made it his duty to show me each time I saw him.'

'I still hate him, you know. Even after everything that happened.' Amara stopped.

'Hate is a hard emotion to keep feeding. I did it for almost all of our marriage.'

'How did you stop, then?'

'I let it go when Harland died and then I withdrew from the memories.'

'And last night you began other memories all of your own. How on earth will this end, Violet?'

'Aurelian de la Tomber is not here this morning on bended knees pleading for my hand in marriage, I am well aware of that. But, his offer of protection for now is enough.'

'Enough?'

Violet laughed and faced her sister-in-law directly. 'You loved your husband, Amaryllis. When he died you mourned him solidly for two years. You are still sad. I, on the other hand, found myself wishing that Harland might have died in the night every day that I awoke while he lived here. When he hit you, Amaryllis, so soon after you arrived at Addington, I understood exactly what sort of a man he was and how none of it was my fault or yours. I never forgave him, but I am trying to forget him.'

'Yet he still haunts us?'

'Well, don't let him do so. Live your life and smile again. Go to Italy and laugh.'

'He may be beautiful, this French Count, and I have never seen you look as fetching as you do this morning, but people are talking of him and it is not all flattering.'

The footman knocked at the door just as Amara finished speaking, announcing that the Minister Mountford had come to call. Violet felt a slight sense of relief that the conversation between them could now be at an end.

Charles looked older this morning than she had ever seen him, his hair a little untidy and the lines under his eyes deep.

'Good morning, ladies. I have come to say that I've purchased your tickets for Italy already, Mrs Hamilton. But before I complete the sale, are you certain you will not also be joining your sister-in-law on holiday, Violet? I would recommend that you do so.'

'I won't be. I would, however, like to thank you for the arranging of guards outside our town house.'

'It was not by my orders.' He stood still as he said this. 'I doubt our office could run to such an expense.'

'Who, then?' Even as she said it she knew the name that would follow.

'The Comte de Beaumont asked me for some recommendations yesterday. He is rumoured to be rich beyond any imagination.'

Violet turned to the window. She did not wish for her godfather to see the emotions that would be so readable in her eyes.

Aurelian de la Tomber had not come, but had sent others in his stead. Was this a sign? Would he stand beside her in any practical manners, but no longer in the intimate ones?

'He is out of London today.'

This brought her attention back into the moment. 'Who is?'

'The Comte. He sent word that he had some business to take care of and would not be in the city until the morrow at least.'

'Do you know what business?' Amaryllis asked this of Charles and Violet blessed her for it.

'Yesterday he saved you at the park, Violet, but only just in the nick of time. De la Tomber does not strike me as a man who would enjoy nearly being bested.'

'What does he strike you as, then?'

'One whom others tread carefully about. If you listen hard, there are many things said of him.'

'I know he is a spy for France.' Violet stated this because she was sure Charles knew he was and because she wanted Amaryllis to know of it, too. 'What else is he?'

'A hidden man. A dealer in violence. A soldier of a ministry that would stop at nothing to see that his home country stays intact.'

'Why did you ask him for his help, then, yesterday?'

'Because he is a man who does not obey the strict rules of conflict. I was right to ask him. Without his presence…'

'Violet would be dead.' Amaryllis stepped forward. 'I am not certain you buried as many whispers as you might have hoped to, though, Mr Mountford. According to our housekeeper, there was much gossip in the markets this morning about the Comte's part in the fracas in Hyde Park.'

'A fact that is worrying.'

'Because it places him in more danger?' These words slipped from Violet unbidden. Already she could see the peril in it, for him, for Aurelian de la

Tomber, her knight in shining armour. Was this part of why he had left London and put other guards in place here? Had he gone now to try to deal with the assailants by himself without the English knowing, in the hidden and festering underbelly of the criminal world?

Would he be back?

She had offered him her body under the pretext of safety, but after last night she knew next time it would be for a repeat of the feelings that he had engendered. She could not imagine there not being a next time, and lust was only a small part of her yearning for him.

Charles looked concerned.

'Everything about the attempt on your life yesterday in the park was unusual, Violet, and made no sense whatsoever. Someone set de la Tomber up and yet it was a last-minute decision on my behalf to visit him and plead for his assistance.'

'Could there be someone in the Home Office who wanted him dealt with, then? Someone with the same information that you had?'

'I received word of the attack an hour or so before it happened so there was no time to gather up a group of youths unless…' He tailed-off, clearly amazed he had actually said so much, but Violet was not letting him off so easily.

'Unless what.'

'Unless the one who sent the assailant wanted the French Comte to be remarked upon, to be out in the open, so to speak?'

'That sounds like a dangerous place to be.'

'It is, but de Beaumont can disappear in a heartbeat just as he can appear in one. He was the one who helped Summerley Shayborne home to England and he has aided countless others.'

'English people?'

'And French and Italian and Spanish. His speciality is dealing with the trickiest of diplomatic disasters and resolving them when it suits those in charge of the power in France. I doubt he has failed in one single mission.'

'Not a man to trifle with, then.'

'Or a man to settle. As your godfather, Violet, I would advise you to stay well away from him.'

Amaryllis coughed in a strange way. 'The French Comte did save her life yesterday, my lord. He can't be all bad.'

'*Untamed* is a better word, Mrs Hamilton. He's like a wolf in a henhouse when he graces the hallowed halls of the *ton*. All teeth and hunger.'

Charles was right in that, Violet thought. Every person in the room was approaching this conversation from a different angle. On her behalf, she wished Aurelian might come back and gobble her up again.

'If there are any developments with your assailant, Violet, I shall send word. As it stands, the guards outside will protect you and Cummings and his department are doing their very best to try and make the miscreant talk.'

'Thank you.' She gave her gratitude in a haze, everything that had happened over the past few days sending her mind awhirl. She wished Aurelian would come tonight to see her, but Charles had said the Comte would not be back in London until tomorrow.

The smell of rivers never changed, Lian thought. Not in Paris nor in London nor in any far-flung stinking hellhole into which he had trawled in order to find information.

The tone of the calls of the working boatmen across a falling day seldom changed, either; the congestion of the evening leaving a heavy wash on the boards of the lighter upon which he travelled.

The others about him pressed in, trying to escape the wetness. Drying heavy wool in winter was difficult and it was far better to simply do away with the need for it. Hence the man to his right was almost plastered to his chest, the smell of old tobacco and cheap liquor on his breath and sharp interest in his eyes.

The note that Violet had showed him last night worried him. The paper had smelt faintly of some scent he could not quite get a hold of. A hand of disguise, but a light hand none the less.

'You be going over for the celebrations of the wedding of the MacKintosh party?'

The man beside him waited for an answer and, having little idea of what he alluded to, Lian simply shook his head. He'd long been at home with accents and had an ear for returning the cadence of languages so the thought of falling into conversation was not worrying him.

What was concerning him was the fire he could

see on the bank to the left, a fierce wind whipping the sparks south into the timbered wall of a shack on the close.

He'd been in the middle of the July fire in Paris of 1810, when the Austrian Ambassador had given a ball to celebrate the wedding of Napoleon to Marie Louise of Austria. Ever since, he'd been wary of flame and this one seemed to be growing by the moment.

Others, too, seemed to be becoming increasingly aware, the shifting weight causing the wherryman to shout at the top of his lungs for the passengers to keep still as the wooden piles of the wharf came beneath the boat.

The air was thick with rancid smoke though the wind was swirling and the next moment it was gone to blow in an opposite direction.

John Wylie was waiting for him.

'We'll need to go away from the riverfront because of the fire.'

'Is it being put out?'

'Oh, aye. The firefighters have arrived and the place is self-standing, so the only problem now is finding a seat in another drinking establishment, given the tavern here has been emptied. I coulda come to you, guv, if ye'd wanted it so.'

Aurelian shook off the idea. 'No. It's better here. Is Welsh with you?' After yesterday at the park he could not be sure he wasn't being watched.

'Over there with Peter Flavell. They both did as ye asked.'

The room they found after walking up the incline

was at the back of the tavern, a small rickety space with the barest of privacy.

'The man in the custody of the Home Office is dead, guv.'

Aurelian swore. 'You are telling me that he died under lock and key and well guarded? That's something to think about and think about hard.'

'Flavell spoke to one of the guards who brought food to the prisoners. He said the man in the bottom cell was dead as a doornail with froth at his mouth come morning.'

'Someone wanted him gone,' Aurelian said as he looked across at Peter Flavell.

'Badly. Douglas Cummings visited him once.'

'Anyone else?'

'A woman. Mrs Antoinette Herbert. She lives in Kensington for I followed her home. A lady of means by the looks and most agitated.'

'You have the address?'

'Here.' Flavell brought a small scrap of paper from his pocket and gave it to him.

'Who was he? The man in gaol?'

'Stephen Miller. A jeweller. He had a small shop in Holborn but he had been Dragoon in the Peninsular Campaign under Moore in Corunna so he was handy with a weapon.'

And cognisant of the properties of gold, Lian thought, trying to put the pieces of the puzzle together.

'There's something else, too.' Frank Welsh spoke now. 'It seems you have stirred up a nest of hornets.

The gaol cell of Miller's might very well be yours to occupy next.'

He smiled. 'I'd like to see them try it. What of Chichester and the death of George Taylor? Did anything more come of that?'

'Taylor was hit by a carriage on the Southern Road. He was another jeweller with a shop in the centre of the city. A well-heeled one, too, by the size of the purse that was found upon him.'

'Not robbery, then?'

'Well, his luggage is missing.'

'Luggage?'

'Taylor had been to Chichester and was on his way back to London, by horse. His steed was found wandering a mile or so up the road and the pub master where he'd been staying was certain he had left with luggage.'

The smell of the fire had reached this place now, the wet scent of damp ash and smouldering embers. At the Austrian Embassy on Chausée d'Antin, Lian had pulled the lifeless body of the Ambassador's wife out of a salon filled with flame and thick black roiling smoke. Fire gave him the feeling of a hollow pit in his stomach, but so did the unexplained deaths of Miller in the gaol and Taylor just outside Chichester.

Desperation caused mistakes and someone willing to kill had a lot to hide. These dead men were not thugs, but jewellers and gentlemen. The man in the boarding house in Brompton Place had been of the same ilk with his soft body and unmarked hands and there had been a full purse in his pocket, too. Men like this should have been enjoying the fruits of their labours rather than dying ignominiously and in violence, yet someone or something was paying them to take a stand.

Douglas Cummings was not quite as he seemed and neither was the jeweller Whitely. This was another worry. Could all these deaths mean that the fortune of French gold was still intact or at least that someone believed it to be? Perhaps the person who had it wanted no others to talk? No links. No strands of culpability. A clear mandate to spend it and never be bothered again.

Violet was the daughter of a jeweller and the wife of a man with French sympathies who had been sent the gold in the first place. Perhaps she knew too much, had seen too much?

'There's something else you need to know, too, guv.' Peter Flavell lowered his voice. 'The woman in the park you saved yesterday was also the one who Douglas Cummings went to see around noon today. He was there for a while. The Minister, Charles Mountford, was there a bit earlier.'

This did not make any sense. Why would Violet meet Cummings at home on the day after an attempt on her life and especially if Mountford had visited an hour or two before him?

The wrong side of the law in a land that was not his own was always going to be a difficult place to operate in. Someone would make a mistake soon, he knew they would and he had to be ready. He just prayed that it was not going to be Violet Addington.

* * *

Hours later Lian watched the Addington town house from a small distance, sliding into the moonlight through the overhanging trees to hide his presence. The same wind that had ignited the shack on the south bank of the Thames blew here, the force of it lifting the old brown leaves from the streets and sending them scurrying down the road towards Beauchamp Place. He glanced at the fob watch at his waist.

Eleven thirty.

Late enough for the house to have gone to bed. He moved forward, waiting till Eli Tucker, the largest of the guards, came closer before speaking.

'Have there been any problems?'

'My God. You gave me a hell of a fright, sir, appearing out of thin air like that. But, no, there hasn't been any sign of trouble.'

'Stay on here, then, until you hear otherwise from me. No one else but me. Do you understand? For I am the one paying your wages and I need you here until I say that I don't.'

'Yes, my lord.'

He left the man there and, using a heavy vine that twisted and knotted, he was up on the second-floor balcony within a moment.

The door opened even as he stood trying to work out exactly what he might say. Violet was dressed in a nightgown, pale and flowing, her hair in the moonlight far darker than it ever looked in the sun.

'Aurelian?'

'I cannot stay.' Hell, what had made him utter that?

Uncertainty, he thought, and the worry that she might begin to understand him just as others did. Distant. Brutal. Savage. Second chances for him were not things easily doled out.

'Why the hell was Cummings here today?'

He had not meant to ask this so baldly, the demand harsh against the candlelight and the quiet.

'He came briefly to deliver some papers.'

Her face flamed and the discomfort in her eyes was easy to see. Lies were his stock in trade and he of all people could recognise untruth.

Flavell had said the man had been in the house for a good hour and he would not have lied. Disappointment filled him even as she stepped forward and her hand took his.

'Come inside for it's freezing out here.'

Her room was so warm he had to take a deep breath, the fire blazing and more than a few candles burning. There were a number of books on a table beside her bed and he tried to remember the last time he'd had enough hours in his life to read. So many things he no longer did as he'd walked the lonely pathways. A ghost sometimes, a shadow. The living embodiment of emptiness. The end of nobody's rainbow.

'Thank you for the guards. They make us feel safer.'

When he didn't answer, the frown on her face settled, but he felt dislocated and strange, the heart of hope ripped from his body.

He was more distant tonight and larger and taller and darker. The clothes he sported were also different, less fashionable. They were garments that the poorer inhabitants of the east side docklands might have favoured. The chill from outside had come in and the fire flickered in the grate and smoked badly. Aurelian smelt of smoke, too, and she wondered. The man from last night had dissolved into this one.

'Your assailant from yesterday is dead.'

Shock ran from her head to her feet. 'How?'

'He either killed himself or someone else did it for him. I do not know which it is yet. My guess is the second.'

No one else had been truly honest with her in all of her life and she liked the way he never tried to soften unwanted facts. It was one of the things about him that she liked the most. He treated her as an equal. The niggle of her own untruth about Cummings's visit surfaced as a result.

Lian said, 'I think that Douglas Cummings may have some hand in this. How long has he been working for Mountford?'

'For years, I should imagine. Why?'

There were tensions in him that she thought he was trying to hide. He spat out Douglas Cummings's name as if he hated the very sound of it.

'A whole lifetime of work and yet he still has no true authority in anything he does. A man like that might seek other avenues of advancement.'

'Illegal avenues?'

'Not everyone is inherently honest.'

'Are you?'

He laughed at that and then sobered. The sound was not kind.

'My father has been placed under home arrest in Paris. He will stay that way for as long as it takes me to find the lost gold.'

'And if you cannot?'

'I very rarely fail in anything I pursue.'

Important considerations and large reasons to succeed, she thought, watching the black indifference in his eyes. There was threat there, too, bound in his words.

'Mountford said the very same thing of you.'

'I don't imagine it was enunciated in a particularly flattering way. We have crossed paths only briefly, the Minister and I, but it has never been easy.'

'He advised me today to keep well away from you.'

'A bit late for that, I think.'

It was the first personal thing he had said to her and she stood still, waiting.

'You probably should take his advice.' His voice was deep and cracked. A voice tonight with a great deal of wariness on its edge.

'Should I?'

His hand slid across the line of her chin though the expression on his face did not match the gentleness of his fingers. There was cider on his breath and in his clothes sat the smell of the river.

'I am not who you think I am, Violet. I am a much darker man than the Comte de Beaumont who appears in society and those who know me also know never to cross me.'

* * *

The shock of his words had her turning. He was a spy who might decipher everything on only small and tiny clues and Amaryllis and her sons would be gone in two days, away from British law and injustice, away from paying so completely for the death of a man who had abused them.

'Cross you? Why would I do that?'

She was glad her voice sounded strong. The fury in her was building by the second, but alongside that came caution.

'Your husband stands right in the very centre of everything. He was a greedy and immoral man by all reports and had been watched by the Home Office here for the last year of his life. They suspected he had French sympathies, though I doubt even Mountford knew the extent that they were a blind for his own bottomless greed.' He stopped for a moment and then went on. 'But perhaps you did and, with your knowledge of gold markings and its properties, you helped him hide it. In ornaments at first and then… somewhere else.'

'You are wrong. Everything you say is wrong.' She hated him at that moment because she had expected so much else from him. Gentleness. Compassion. Thankfulness after a whole night of loving.

'If I were to further guess at the truth of your fear, I'd say it's because you weren't the person who really killed Harland Addington in the stables. I imagine, however, it *was* you who then led the most difficult stallion into the stall. After doing that you would have gathered the murder weapon and, using the cover of darkness, thrown it as far as you could into the lake at the foot of the gardens before the manor.'

The thought hit Violet then that Aurelian de la Tomber was like no other at all. No wonder he had walked through Europe unchallenged with a mind that could place all the small disparate variables of life into one whole and perfect pattern. Amaryllis's future sat so firmly in the palm of his hand it made her feel sick.

'You are wrong, my lord, in your summations and I want you to leave.'

For now this was all that she had, this chance of distance. Two days till Amaryllis took ship to Rome. Forty-eight hours before her sister-in-law's safety was assured.

She was pleased when he tipped his head and did just as she had asked.

Aurelian watched Cummings's house for the rest of the night, perched in the space between a stone wall and a small evergreen. He'd learned how to sit still and focus for as many hours as he needed to, a training honed in the harsher war zones of Napoleon's push into Spain. To block everything out, except for specific visual and observation skills, required effort. With such a quiet and solitary life, he often felt others saw only the danger in him, the softer parts lost in the expectations of intelligence.

He blocked out the fury of Violet's untruths. Sex was a double-edged sword after all, for it cleaved the body together while leaving the mind open to question.

Why had she offered her body to him yesterday and why had he come into her arms with such relief? The light around her was a part of it, that he knew, but there was also distrust burning between them. Untruth had a certain sound and he'd heard it many a time.

He'd peered in the downstairs window, too, before he had climbed the vine and noticed that the ornament was gone, another ivory bust in its place. The portrait of Harland had been replaced, as well, a peaceful rural scene resting in its stead.

She'd been prickly and distant tonight, but she was also as sensual as hell. The nightgown she had been wearing hugged her bosom, outlining generous breasts and a thin waist. It had been an effort to look away and then leave when all he had wanted to do was take her and be damned any consequences. He shook his head at the thought and concentrated on the job at task.

Having slept in fifteen-minute quotas, he woke into stillness and in the very early morning the door to Cummings's quarters opened and a woman stepped out. Alone. A carriage collected her, a conveyance with two well-bred horses, a driver and a footman. Every detail was noted. Her dark hair, the walk, her voice as she bade the man on the box to take her home.

The time of departure pointed to a liaison and her face was imprinted on his mind as he sifted through memory. Peter Flavell had mentioned a woman of means in the company of Miller. The dice rolled into

place. Too many clues to be simply chance, for he
was sure that this was Mrs Antoinette Herbert and
he would visit her later in the day. It was past time to
break this game wide apart to see in which direction
the rats scurried for cover.

Aurelian took a hackney to the house in Kensington in the early afternoon after a quick snatched hour
of sleep.

Mrs Herbert was sitting in her downstairs parlour,
drinking a fine brandy, when he was shown through
by her butler. She was not as young as he might have
thought initially and she did not look in the slightest
bit surprised as he gave her his name.

'You expected me?'

'I had heard you were here in London and I imagined you might visit.'

'It's your association with Stephen Miller I hold interest in, Mrs Herbert. You went to see him in gaol?
Why?'

'He was a lover.' She sat back at that and laughed.
'I have shocked you, I think.'

His eyes ran across the pages on her desk filled
with writing and he shook his head.

'It takes a lot to shock me, madam.'

What was she telling him? There were things here
he could not quite decipher.

'Why are you here?'

Her expression changed with these words, the blue
eyes darkening and the lines around her mouth much
more noticeable. Not a beauty, but handsome none

the less. Placing her question aside, he countered with one of his own.

'Where is it you were born?'

'In Normandy and I have heard your name mentioned on many different occasions, Comte de Beaumont, though some of the rumours are not so favourable.' She sat up and took a large sip of her brandy.

'I remember your name, from before, too. You are a supporter of Napoleon Bonaparte and you hold out the hope of French supremacy in Europe.'

'I was told you were quick.'

'Were you also told what brings me here?'

'I imagine it is to trace the lost French gold? Perhaps I should tell you right now that I was one of those who contributed to its largesse.'

'A close association, then, considering you were Lord Addington's lover, too.'

This time the blood left her face and she stood with all the care of someone who needed a table to support them.

'Viscount Addington was a fool and his untimely death was not such a surprise.'

'Because without him you could reclaim the gold for Napoleon? You knew where some of it was, after all, and if getting your hands on it required another lover, then...' He left the implication hanging.

'Politics makes mockery of the small vanities of men.'

'And your beliefs are the only legitimate ones?' He laughed even as he meant not to, but fools like Antoinette Herbert had filled the greater part of his life in intelligence and he was tired of it.

'I will give you a warning first, Mrs Herbert. Any further attempts on the life of Lady Addington will be met by me with a response that you could never recover from.'

'Get out.'

'With pleasure.'

He left and walked all the way to Green Park, needing the cold and the silence and the empty landscape to calm down his anger.

Antoinette Herbert had a part in the deaths and threats and violence, he was certain of it. She could have had no direct part in the killing of George Taylor, for she had not left the city boundaries since the second week of January, the day after he was shot.

The cards were forming a pattern and the haphazard facts were falling into shape. He would have her watched and she would know of it, a quiet message of intent in such surveillance.

Mrs Herbert liked jewellery, her neck embellished by two strands of heavy gold and both wrists and ears sporting more. Her brandy was French. Illegally procured given the customs ban on such goods and he knew this vintage had only been cleared from the maker in the last year.

The picture was building and widening out.

A house newly painted. Clothes of the latest fashion. The sweat beading on her upper lip when he had mentioned the name of Viscount Addington. That had been a guess and a good one, too. There were other things he might have mentioned, as well.

Albert Herbert, her husband, had died in suspicious circumstances, falling from a horse on the road north of Lyon. Since then she had enjoyed an array of disparate lovers. A woman who gathered men to her like a black widow spider, spinning nets around opportunities.

A woman who might use her lovers as bait as she tried to hide a cache of hidden gold? She'd told him she had been one of the contributors in the attempt to oust a legitimate English Government.

A dangerous confession that seemed out of place and foolish. But Antoinette Herbert was no dullard and he would have to watch her carefully.

Chapter Eight

Violet saw Aurelian at a ball the day after Amaryllis had gone. Her guards were all still in place so that she knew he had not abandoned her entirely which was gratifying. The want and ache of her body for him wasn't ebbing, but growing to a proportion where she could think of nothing else save him being inside her again. She was swollen with the need, breathless with it sometimes, all the moments of each day focused on appearing normal and sane.

Had he made her crazy with his instructions on the intimate arts? She longed for moonlight and nakedness and the way he took her mouth under his to make her forget the world and yet thought perhaps it would never happen again.

'You are pensive tonight, Violet. I heard your sister-in-law has gone on an extended visit to Italy. Do you miss her?'

Antonia MacMillan next to her asked the question softly.

'I do. The house seems very empty without her and the boys.'

'You did not think to go with them?'

'I mulled it over and then decided now was not quite the right time.' Perhaps she should have simply cut her ties and left. Perhaps it was unwise, all this futile hope of something more between her and Aurelian de la Tomber, especially given the anger between them that seemed as prevalent as the lust.

Gregory MacMillan had come to stand beside them, his stock tied in a fashion that looked most complicated.

'I hope that you will, as the most beautiful woman in the room, dance with me this evening, Lady Addington.'

Antonia admonished him with her fan. 'I am not sure how to take that dismissal, brother. Were I more sensitive I might now never speak to you again.'

The arrival of a small group at the far end of the salon caught everyone's attention. Aurelian de la Tomber flanked by the Lords Luxford and Thornton had people turning.

Tonight the waistcoat and jacket he wore were embroidered in fine black thread to create a pattern across the wool. He was a man whose ancient and aristocratic lineage showed across every line in his face and body and so very different from the one who had smiled down at her on her bed at her town house, his naked body bathed in moonlight.

She knew he saw her, though he did not come

closer, a tight bunch of people in his vicinity keeping them talking.

Perhaps it was best that way after the fiasco in the park. The Earl of Thornton and Viscount Luxford were men of reputation in their own right and any gossip about Aurelian would as likely founder with the strength of their family ties supporting him. Perhaps that was why he had come, for surely of all men he would know how to use and sway society with ease.

It was a good half an hour later when Summerley Shayborne approached her. She had met both him and his beautiful wife at one or two of the smaller private social soirées earlier in the Season. Rumour had it that they had escaped back to Luxford Manor in Sussex as soon as was feasible and seldom left the place. The Major had been lauded on the Continent for being irreplaceable as Sir Arthur Wellesley's first officer of intelligence and as such he was a hero here in England of the very first degree.

Up close he was as tall as Aurelian and almost as beautiful.

'It is a pleasure to meet you again, Lady Addington. I hear you know my friend, Aurelian de la Tomber. It seems you have made quite an impression upon him.'

She blushed, something she could rarely remember doing before.

Antonia was observing her strangely, her eyes questioning, and Violet felt as if all the lies she had built to stand on were suddenly shattering beneath her feet.

Since arriving in London she had been in control of everything, showing others only what she wanted them to see. People liked her, admired her even, her resilience lauded and remarked upon.

No one understood the demons that lived inside and the constant nervous worry. The worry of being found out and pulled up before the courts, the wife of a man who was anything but careful in his dealings outside of the law. The worry, too, of losing even the roof over her head and no one else in the world to truly ask for help.

'The Comte saved my life in Hyde Park four days ago. Did he tell you that?'

'He did.'

'The thing is, my lord, that I think he has placed himself in danger by doing so.'

Shayborne laughed at this. 'If anyone can handle danger, I imagine it would be him.'

Other women had joined the group around Aurelian now, each more beautiful than the last, Antonia among them. 'It seems that you may be right, Lord Luxford, for he has no shortage of admirers here.'

The Viscount looked straight at her, which was disconcerting. 'I hear you also saved him a few weeks back from freezing to death one cold and snowy night?'

'Well, perhaps it was not quite as dire as you say.' She could feel Gregory MacMillan at her back, listening. 'I picked him up outside the Barringtons' ball and delivered him home.'

Shayborne tipped his head and smiled.

'He is a man who needs good friends, I think, and I am gladdened that you are one.'

With that he moved off, with an air of solidness and certainty. As people watched him she wondered just exactly what his wife, Celeste, was like under the surface, for she could not imagine the Viscount with anyone ordinary.

Moving herself, she made for the side of the room to glance out of the tall and balconied windows hung tonight with wreaths of greenery. She knew the second that Aurelian joined her, a heightened sense of excitement coursing through her body as she saw his reflection in the window.

Out of the earshot of the others he leaned down across her. 'I hope you are well, Lady Addington?'

The formality of her name made her frown.

'I think I have been better, my lord.' She was tired of pretending. 'I had heard that you'd left town altogether.'

'Hardly.'

She suddenly did not know quite how to handle this. His arm touched hers where they stood, the shock of connection burning across uncertainty.

'I missed you.' His words. Unexpected.

All the people around them simply fell away, into the mist. It was as if it was only they and the music floating around the room.

'I missed you, too.'

She could not hold it in, this honesty that admitted far too much.

The tune swirled, the colours of silks and satins blending. Her own dress was part of it, as well, the lace was embellished with something she herself had sewn on just last night. Aurelian's hand pressed against the small of her back and she could feel each finger there.

'Would you dance with me?'

When she nodded he led her on to the floor. She could feel a wave of notice all around her, the buzz of conversation loud. His hand came into hers then as he brought her around to face him.

'My sister-in-law departed for Italy yesterday.'

He breathed out hard. She could feel the air against the top of her head even as he said nothing.

Come tonight and find me, Aurelian. Come and show me all the things that you did before.

'You will be safe alone. I have seen to it.'

Only this. Disappointment blossomed.

Why the hell had he just told her he missed her? It had slipped out unbidden as soon as he had touched her arm, her aloneness worrying him.

She wore the same dress he had seen her in when she had picked him up off the road in Brompton Place, but this time a different lace had been sewn across the bodice. He could make out the catch of stitches in the light. A new question. A further oddness. If Violet had been the one to hide a veritable fortune in gold, she would hardly need to be so penny pinching in her choice of clothing.

God, the questions kept coming and now here in

the most unlikely of settings came a new realisation that even if she were the perpetrator behind the lost gold he would protect her.

From everyone.

'Did you find out more of George Taylor?' Her query startled him.

'His luggage was stolen on the road south after he left Chichester. A robbery would allow his death some sense. Gold, while heavy, is still a portable fortune and, should you wish, easy to hide away from the notice of others.'

'Are you implying someone has?'

He began to laugh. 'If they have, my advice to them would be to mind their backs. The French gold has made corpses of many so far, but people always leave clues. In my job it's one of the first things you ever learn.'

Violet thought that his eyes looked like a hawk angling for its prey and she shivered with the realisation.

The camaraderie in her bedroom at the town house in Chelsea seemed replaced by a more brittle regard and a wariness that held the scent of suspicion. His body was like a stringed instrument tuned in to danger, every small nuance noted and vibrating against truth.

Had he learnt something of Harland's proclivity to hurt others? Could he have found out more of her husband's death in the stables of Addington or of her part in it? There had been a misstep between them, but she could not quite understand where it had happened.

Whatever it was, the distance between them seemed heightened, quivering under the pressure of what was known and what was not.

As the orchestra ground to a halt, however, she could do nothing more than follow him to rejoin Major Lord Shayborne who watched them from one side of the room. She was glad that Antonia and her brother had moved away in the interim.

Every time she met Aurelian de la Tomber she was upended and more than surprised. She almost expected it now, this topsy-turvy uncertainty. When he excused himself to find them a drink, Summerley Shayborne was quick to speak.

'Lian is the only man in the world who I trust implicitly, but he has been hurt before and I should not wish to see him be so yet again.'

Somehow Violet did not think Shayborne meant the physical scars. No, these words were being given to her as a warning.

'My wife says he should marry and settle down. She thinks all men reach that point where home is paramount.' His glance travelled across the room to where Aurelian stood.

Such an observation had her heartbeat rising and she wondered suddenly how much he might have told Shayborne about her fractured past.

But Viscount Luxford did not seem to regard her in the way of a foe. Instead there was some odd notice there that she could not quite put her finger on.

Overcome by her thoughts, Violet excused herself. She needed to be away for a few moments in a place of silence and calm. Seeing the Comte besieged by women here worried her, for there were many in society who would have made admirable wives. Perhaps Summerley Shayborne did know of his friend's plans and was not saying.

Violet had always been so careful to keep suitors at a distance until Aurelian de la Tomber. Until he had swept her off her feet and made her into a woman she barely recognised.

She had reached the ladies' retiring room now and sat down on a chair propped beneath the window. Outside it was snowing and the night looked cold and dark. Lady Elizabeth Grainger suddenly appeared from nowhere, her eyes full of interest.

'I was just saying to my friend Lady Drayton that you are looking very fetching lately, Lady Addington. I do hope the incident in the park the other day has not continued to upset you.'

'I am well, thank you, and that person has been dealt with.'

'By the Comte de Beaumont?'

'Mr Mountford and Mr Cummings also helped,' she added, trying to form a layer of legitimacy around Aurelian's actions.

'I saw Douglas Cummings in Chichester a few weeks back and he looked most agitated. He is not a man with the propensity to hide his feelings, unlike the French Comte who manages it beautifully. Were I a young girl again I think I might be joining the ranks of others here in the hope of knowing him better.' She stopped. 'He watches you when you are not looking and I gather he is more than interested in what he sees.'

'I am a widow, Lady Grainger, and no longer young. There is not much to see.'

'You sell yourself short, my dear. You have endured one marriage to a man no one could stand and emerged out the other end of it almost intact. I salute you in that.'

This time Violet smiled. The woman was so undiplomatic it was almost refreshing and she'd heard that Elizabeth Grainger was neither a tittle-tattle nor a gossip.

'I knew de la Tomber's mother once. She was the kind of woman whom people were drawn to. Very much like yourself, in actual fact, and unconscious of it. The true and great beauties are always like that, I told my sister just the other night after seeing you and de Beaumont in the park.'

Flabbergasted at such praise Violet sat still, relieved when another of the woman's friends came in to join them and she could escape.

She could not actually believe that such compliments were in any way deserved, but the elderly woman's words had been sincere in their delivery and they had warmed her heart.

Aurelian de la Tomber had disappeared by the time she returned to the ballroom and it was not long before she also made her goodbyes.

Lady Elizabeth's summation of the character of Douglas Cummings was also interesting and the

Chichester connections rang alarm bells for this was the city near which George Taylor had been murdered and the timings were similar.

Was she imagining things that were not there and finding straws of guilt where none existed? She wished she could speak alone to Aurelian and tell him of her conjectures because of all the men in the world she knew he was the one who could make sense of them.

She awoke in the early hours of the morning to find him there standing at her window and looking out.

'I wanted to make certain you'd arrived home safely and I had not said goodbye.'

'Perhaps because you were besieged by women and they had your whole attention.' This was petty, she knew, but she could not take it back.

He simply laughed.

'I sat in the ladies' retiring room for half an hour where I was waylaid by Lady Elizabeth Grainger.' Sitting up, she straightened the bed sheets around her.

'The older woman at the park the other day?'

Violet nodded. 'She told me that if she had been many years younger she may have set her cap at you. She also said that she saw Douglas Cummings in Chichester two weeks or so ago.'

'About the same time that George Taylor was killed?'

'Charles placed my assailant in Douglas Cummings's custody. He was the man with the responsibility to keep him alive.'

'One of the gaolers I talked to said they were told to

go home early. He also said that the man who assaulted you had been a soldier, but had become a jeweller.'

'You have already been investigating this?'

'Stephen Miller had a jewellery shop in Holborn.'

'Taylor was a jeweller, too.'

'And your husband dealt in the questionable realms of gold tampering. Do you see a pattern?'

She did. It was the gold that brought them all together and greed that had torn them apart.

'I am a jeweller's daughter and I think that Harland's enemies have put two and two together and deduced that it is me who has stolen the gold.'

'And did you?'

'If you truly need to ask me that, Aurelian, you should not be here.'

'Then where do you think it went?'

She swallowed as she gave him her answer. 'I think Harland took some to fund his gambling debts and then he lost control of the rest when he tried to hide it.'

'George Taylor and Stephen Miller took it over?'

'There were others, too.'

'Who? Who else was in it?'

'Charles Mountford asked me that. I said I didn't know. The jeweller Whitely, perhaps?'

He waited for a moment. Good intelligence was never to be rushed. It required patience and trust as well as luck and all the time in the world.

'The thing is I did find a list of initials. There were five names underlined twice in dark pen on a sheet of paper and stuffed in a crack of wood in Harland's desk.'

'Was D.C. among them?'

'Yes.'

'Who else?'

'George Taylor and three other initials that I could not find a correlation for at the time.'

'Where is the list?'

'I buried it at Addington Manor under the roses in a tin box. Then the place was sold and I did not think to retrieve it.'

'Who were the others?'

'S.M. was one of them.'

'Stephen Miller? Who else?'

'A.W. and J.C. Then there was a blank line with only an *A* written on it.'

'Did you show it to anyone else at all?'

She shook her head. 'It seemed a dangerous thing to do.'

'Don't tell, then, not even Charles Mountford. I am not sure how far he would go to make sure you really are safe.'

'He wanted me to go to Rome.'

Lian tried to school his face, but she must have seen something for all the blood simply drained from hers.

'It is a trap?'

'I don't know. To be sure I had Amaryllis Hamilton and the children rerouted.'

'To where?'

'Greece. My family has a house there. They will want for nothing and her letters will come through me to you.'

'It's more than the gold you are searching for, isn't it?'

'Treason sets men to lengths that seem unmeasurable, but I think Mountford is trying to do his best under difficult circumstances. I just don't know how secure his office is. The first objective of my *ministère* is to retrieve the gold, but the British Government and the Home Office are much more interested in the names of those who had some hand in treason here.'

'You think it's Cummings? You think he is the one behind it?'

'In the park he saw the man who tried to kill you and directed his men in the opposite direction. At the time that made no sense, but now...' He tailed-off. 'He also visited you at your town house the day after the incident in Hyde Park and you told me he had not. Why?'

Turning away, Violet walked to the window, pulling the curtains back and looking out. Her reflection showing in the glass made her seem slight and still.

'Douglas Cummings came to plead for my hand in marriage.'

'*Merde.*'

She spun around at that and faced him directly. 'I said no and he was furious and I suppose I thought his feelings were hurt so...'

'You didn't want to tell me of it.'

'It seemed...tarnished. He tried to kiss me. Then he began to cry.'

'Come with me to Sussex, Violet. My house there is safe and I can watch for enemies. We could leave in the morning.'

'Why? Why would you do this for me?'

He stopped her words by placing his fingers across her lips and feeling the breath of the words falter.

'I was married once a long time ago and my wife died when I failed to protect her. But I can protect you for we can be married tomorrow. I procured a special licence three days ago just in case.'

'Married?' The word wound around them. He had not asked. He had not wanted her opinion. He'd merely told her without giving her any inkling whatsoever about what was going on in his head or in his heart. A pragmatic proposal to assuage the earlier guilt of his wife's passing. Nothing more?

'You do not think we can continue on like this, surely, Violet, without…?' His glance went to the bed. 'What if I get you with child?'

Should she tell him of her barrenness? Could she?

With absolute care she told him something else entirely. 'I married Harland a month after meeting him and I regretted it by the time the second month rolled around.'

The anger in her words was very easy to hear, but she did not care for it was a sorrow she had never learnt to bear, her stupidity and hopeless rush. 'So it is not a state I wish to enter into again. But—' her bruised eyes directly met his own '—I shall not refuse to come to your bed without it.'

He gave the impression he was shocked into silence.

'You are the most dangerous spy in all of Europe and one people steer well clear of so as not to incite your wrath. Every story I have heard of you is more audacious and risky than the last. The opium dens. The underground ministry in Paris. An easy disposal of enemies. Your job of crossing between enemy lines and dealing with situations that no one else can. Yet you are mortified at the thought of the union of our bodies without the blessing of a marriage certificate. Why?'

'Because I cannot keep your enemies at bay without giving you my name.'

'Just as I cannot protect you if I agree to this.'

'Protect me?'

She turned away to the window and breathed in hard. 'I was the one who asked George Taylor to fashion the first ornament. Harland was gambling far beyond his means and I thought it was family money he played with and lost. Amaryllis and the boys deserved something left and so I made the decision to make sure there was an inheritance.'

'Lord.'

'I came across him piling up gold coins one day, carelessly, and told him it would be better to fashion what he was not using into a statue. That way no one would know of its value except him and it could be melted down when he needed it. He liked the idea and asked me to pursue it, but George Taylor, the jeweller, was a man I should not have entrusted with my mission. A quarter of the gold went into the piece of art and the rest was of silver and lead. I put away the unused gold and told Amaryllis of my plan, but George Taylor came to Harland and let him know what I had done. My husband punished me and then proceeded to continue the charade for his own benefit with gold that was sent over to him from France. There were three more ornaments made.'

'How did he punish you?'

'With his fists. With a strap. With the things that husbands across the ages have beaten their wives with. Needless to say he also took the gold.'

'Where were your parents?'

'Dead. I was not allowed to contact anyone outside Addington Manor. I had been forbidden to take a horse out or a carriage. I was watched by Harland's servants from dawn to dusk and any new disobedience was swiftly dealt with. In the end fright kept me numb and Harland began to stay away from our estate for longer and longer periods of time which suited me.'

She raised her eyes to his.

'I am ruined well and truly, don't you see, Aurelian? Tonight in the ballroom you had the choice of every available woman there and there were many young and beautiful candidates. Your friend Summerley Shayborne said as much to me. It can be this and no more.' There were tears in her eyes as she said it, thinking of her barrenness and her inability to ever produce an heir. 'It is all that I can offer you. My body.'

'Then it is enough.'

He pushed her nightdress down across her shoulders and one hand came beneath her left breast to cup the weight of it. When he lifted it to his mouth she breathed in.

The rug beneath them was thick and warm, his shirt and neckcloth off even as he brought her down.

Flame licked in the fireplace, the eddies of their movements inciting it, and the room from this angle was strange and different. Here the night was close and the morning far. Here the thrall of all she had felt before returned.

This lust or truth or whatever it was, this nameless thing wrapped in the forbidden, was fashioned in nearly honesty, too, now, with the secrets between them lessened.

Her fingers traced his cheek and she opened her eyes to watch him, a puzzlement there.

'What?' She whispered this, their lips still touching, just a breath of words but heard none the less.

'You are beautiful.'

Her forefinger then ran across the bridge of his brow, smoothing the lines, making him smile.

'And brave,' he continued, 'and kind.'

Tears pooled and ran down her cheeks. It had been a long time since anyone had said anything so very tender to her, yet tonight she could almost believe them to be true.

When his lips nuzzled her breast again she arched her neck and smiled, at his exuberance and his expertise, his hands stroking, his flesh warm. A skilled lover with a thousand things to teach her.

'I can hear you thinking, Violet.' He whispered this in her ear.

'I want to remember how you do it, how you make me want you.'

'Why?'

'So I can give you the gift back.'

She felt him smile against her skin. 'This between us? There are no repayments needed.'

His hand had fallen to her stomach now, arching in circles that were ever expanding. She felt her breath hitch as he dipped lower.

'Relax, my love, and just feel.' Such an endearment was unexpected and she bit down on a reply.

Love me, Aurelian. Let me forget. Take me to a place where it is only us.

Her hands clung to him even as his fingers came within her, potent and life-giving, catching her between this world and another one as the broken edges of her life softened. She was no match for him, no match for all the things that he knew, but his grace was surprising.

He would not take that which she did not wish to give, he would not hurt her, either. She could feel her wetness on his fingers and wondered at the way her body rose upwards seeking release, finding the place where thought turned into feeling. Then she was there riding the waves, understanding the elation, breathless and fluid, closing her eyes tight and looking inwards.

She was like no other woman he had been with. She was elemental and earthy as much as she was refined and careful. Such opposites attracted him and made him wonder how many more secrets were inside waiting to be discovered. He undid his breeches front with an unbecoming haste.

'My turn now.'

He was in her quickly, the finesse he was lauded for lost under desperation as he came. God, he was like a green boy fumbling in anxiety, pumping in as if he had never lain with anyone before. His mouth came down across hers, sealing the sounds he might make into silence, claiming home.

Violet had him imagining things he had not ever thought of before. The cross at his neck hung between them and he vowed to remove it when he got back to the town house. Veronique was gone, but she had never branded him like Violet Addington did, never made him fretful and impatient, anxious and worried. He wanted to bundle her up here and now and place her into his coach to race through what was left of the night to Sussex. He wanted to wrap her in isolation safe from those who might hurt her, away from the gathering forces of greed and politics that he was so much a part of.

'There is a finality in making love, isn't there?' Her words were soft and he smiled before speaking.

'*La petite mort*, we call it in France. The little death in a brief weakening of consciousness. Some never feel it.'

Her hand came up and she stroked the skin on his cheek, cradling his face. 'I did not…before.'

The yearning in her words made him sad.

'Let me take you to a luncheon tomorrow at Wake's. It is a private hotel in Brook Street.'

He should not ask this, he knew, after her refusal for his hand in marriage. His personal life would always be overshadowed by his professional one and any vulnerability would be noticed. But he wanted for once to feel…normal. A man who might take his woman somewhere beautiful and elegant and discreet, to dine together as if no demons lapped at their heels.

'I would like that.'

A log in the fire shifted, sending sparks across the back of the grate, and they both looked over at it.

'When I was young I used to imagine fairies lived in flame. My mother had hair the same colour as mine and she told me that they did.'

'What happened to her?'

'She died in childbirth along with my baby brother. He was called John.'

'And your father?

'He married again shortly after. I think my new stepmother wished it was only Papa and her in the marriage for I was ten at the time and…difficult.'

'How?'

'In all the ways a girl might be who had just lost her beloved mother. They sent me off to boarding school in Bath and after that I was seldom home.'

'So you were lonely?'

When she shifted position a lock of her hair fell across the side of her face. The colour always surprised him and he lifted the curl of it away from her eyes.

'"It is observed that the red haired of both sexes are more libidinous and mischievous than the rest, whom yet they may exceed in strength and activity.'"

She smiled and watched him directly. 'Where is that from? I think I have heard it before.'

'Jonathan Swift's *Gulliver's Travels*. Summerley Shayborne and I devoured that book at school. I think he might be right, by the way.'

'Who?'

'Swift. You are libidinous and mischievous and strong.'

'Aurelian.'

'Yes, Violet?'

'Make love to me again.'

'Ah, my red-headed libidinous lady, that I will.'

The following day when he came to escort her to Wake's Hotel he looked more beautiful than she had ever seen him. Dressed in his city clothes, the green of his jacket brought out the gold of his eyes and slim-fitting breeches showed off the line of his legs.

In the early afternoon among company it was if they were different people altogether, her hand on his sleeve, his courtly manners, the way she could barely glance at him without feeling how he had made her feel when he was inside her.

The waiters ushered them to an alcove near the double-sashed front windows. Outside it was grey and cold. Inside, though, the burgundy of the plush decor added a warmth and a richness.

'I hope you will enjoy the meal, Violet.'

Aurelian's words were quiet and she saw him glance around to take in the faces of the other three or four couples. He sat against the wall, side on, his chair tilted to the room. A place where he could see everything that went on around him.

'It looks lovely.'

The waiter had come with a bottle of wine and he spoke of its recommendations at length. 'It's French,' Aurelian explained after the waiter left. 'From the Luberon, a region where the sun shines always. I know it well for my family has land there.'

The de la Tombers were as wealthy as Antonia had proclaimed them to be and that fact worried Violet. Almost every pound she had salvaged from her marriage to Harland had gone into retaining the town house in Chelsea. She was existing now on the crumbs of money left and, apart from a small amount of jewellery, she had little to her name. She could never have afforded to come to eat at a place like this.

The bubble of pleasure shivered somewhat and she took in a deep breath. She was ruined in so many ways that it made no sense at all for Aurelian to be here. Courting her.

She could see others in the room watching them, or watching him, a man who looked as if he was born to the high life. Why had he detoured and become a spy? What had made him turn his back on a life of ease?

'I was relieved when my husband died.' It slipped out unbidden, this travesty, and could not be taken back.

'Relieved enough to take the blame for his passing?'

She did not answer.

'I told you of my wife and how I failed to protect her. She was drowned in the river. What I did not say was that Veronique was with a lover at the time, a friend whom we both knew. A man who decided if he could not have her permanently then no one else would.'

'Where is this man now?'

'Dead.'

'By your hand?'

'No. By his own. He found a pistol and shot himself the day her body was brought up from the Seine.'

These secrets he gave were welcomed because she saw in them a distance she understood.

'I found survival in a cause after that, the cause of freedom and justice and Napoleon Bonaparte's New France. For even now knowing all that he wasn't, he was still a man of bravery. He wanted the people who'd been disenfranchised by history to rise up again and take their allotment in what was owed. He wanted the power himself, too, of course, the new leader of a changing France.'

'What of the aristocratic de Lorraine-Lillebonnes? Were they to be a part of this new guard, too?'

'I think my father was too caught in the old ways of privilege and would have found it difficult to have given away any rights. As for me? I have walked in my job in both the camps of plenty and of poverty and once you do that it is impossible not to understand that people are all the same really. They want food and shelter and an occupation that is honourable. They want a dream, too, and the chance for more. And they need to love. A spouse, children, family, a place. To love well is to belong.'

His words sent a chill across her. She had never loved well or been loved or belonged. Her mother had died when she was ten and her father and his new wife had found her to be a nuisance. Harland had not loved her, either, despite his proclamations of doing so in the first month of their courtship. He'd loved money. He'd loved his position in society. He'd coveted more of both and tried to use her to obtain it until he'd realised he couldn't and so he had thrown her away, too.

Amaryllis Hamilton was the closest she had ever come to loving since losing her mother, a woman who mourned a husband taken too soon and whose poor financial position had made it imperative that she seek shelter at her family home of Addington.

'Once I thought I'd be a famous jeweller. I dreamed of necklaces and rings and bracelets wrought from the purest gold imaginable. When I mustered the courage to show Papa the designs I'd drawn in my journal he only laughed. He said that it was foolish to want things one could never have and that I would be married before the summer was out and happy with babies and a great house to run. I truly think that he believed this. He made me believe it, too.'

She swallowed and made herself carry on. 'Harland took what was left of delight away from me in his way, as well, and tarnished it with his endless greed. And now…' she swallowed '…now there is only shame left, shame that I should have been the one to lead him into the temptation of counterfeit. Hundreds of years of honesty spoiled in a heartbeat, the gold markings

I had always loved blemished and stained. An unre-coverable sin.'

The wine glass in Aurelian's hand reflected in the lights above them. She could tell he was measuring his response.

'Nothing is ever as you might think it. My father wanted me to take over the estates in Normandy be-cause he himself once thought that farming and an agricultural life might have made him happy. My grandmother wanted me to become a husband and a father and live in the apartments on the Rue Saint-Honoré near to her. Mama was more complex. She hoped I'd renounce my French heritage and move to the English countryside and a manor house that was hers by right of inheritance. She worried for me and my future in Paris even as she loved my father.' He smiled. 'Every person has their own particular belief system, you see, formed by what has made them the happiest.'

'What has that been for you? Your happiest times?' She asked this even as she tried to think of an answer for herself. The sad thing was she could not really re-member a time when she had felt truly joyous except for the nights when she'd lain in the arms of Aurelian de la Tomber.

'Maybe right now, sitting here with you and watch-ing how the light falls on the red of your hair. Perhaps that is the trick of life, Violet. Enjoying the moment.'

She liked his answer. For so long she had been afraid and lonely and disappointed. Yet now in the aftermath of true peril she saw a glimmer of hope.

The velvet seats were comfortable and she could smell the meals of the other patrons as they were brought out. There was music close, too, and the snow that had threatened to fall all morning was suddenly thick outside, like a wonderland scene in a book she had bought once for Amara in the shop at the end of Regent Street.

She had never sat and talked like this with anyone before. Aurelian felt safe and dangerous, foreign and known. He felt like a man who was solid even though he existed in shadows.

'Gregory MacMillan said that you were seen frequenting an opium den here in London.'

'And you are asking if I am a patron?'

'Yes.' Her directness surprised her, but she didn't drop her gaze.

'George Taylor was a member there and I wanted to find out more of him. I seldom locate the people I am looking for in more salubrious circumstances. In fact, the opium den was tame.'

'And the boarding house on Brompton Place?'

'I'd been sent a message to meet a man there who had information pertaining to the lost French gold. He tried to kill me as soon as I arrived.'

'So you killed him instead?'

He leaned forward and looked her straight in the eye. 'I am not giving you excuses, Violet, only the truth.'

'And I thank you for it.'

The waiter had returned now with a small list of the day's meals. It was strange, this juxtaposition of the ordinary and the extraordinary, for she could feel every part of her body alive in a way it had not been before. Harland had palmed her off with mistruths. Aurelian did not.

'I will be away for the next few days. A contact who had connections to your husband has agreed to talk with me. My guards will protect you here.'

'You think it is that dangerous?'

'I hope not, but it is best to be sure. When I return, Summerley Shayborne has asked me down to his estate of Luxford and I hoped you might join me? I think it would be good for you to get out of London for a few days.'

'I would like that.'

He smiled and she knew then why many women in society had fallen so markedly at his feet. Harland's beauty had been skin-deep and he had been a vain man. Aurelian de la Tomber, on the other hand, was much more than his clothes and his appearance. He was dangerous to be sure but he was honest with it. When he told her things, it would be the truth. She could barely believe the relief that came with such a knowledge.

'How is your hand?' It was still bandaged but more lightly now, the dark of his skin showing up against white.

'Compared to all the other injuries I have had in the past it is a mere scratch.'

Looking down he began to twist the heavy signet ring off his finger.

'I want you to keep this on you, Violet. If at any

time you feel threatened, drop the ring somewhere others can find it and I will come.'

The warmth of the gold sat on her palm, the crest easily seen in the light of the room. She had sent this back to him the first time but now her fingers curled around it.

'This is the best I can offer at the moment.'

'Offer?' She could not understand what he meant.

'My protection. Reputations like mine are useful sometimes. What was the weapon you held in your left pocket the other day at the park?'

Her mouth simply fell open. 'How would you know of that?'

'I watched you. There is much to be seen in the unspoken.'

Throwing caution to the wind she found another question. 'What do you see in me now?'

'You are not quite certain whether or not you have a serpent by its tail or by its teeth for you cannot understand how I know things and that worries you. But, the overriding emotion that shows on your face is relief. You want my body and you want to give me yours. Perhaps because you felt nothing with Harland and perhaps because I make you forget. I can live with those emotions because I understand them both.'

She looked as if she might cry, the tears in her eyes pooling and her glance falling away from his own. She looked little and lost and puzzled, a woman who was beautiful beyond belief and yet did not realise it.

His mother had had the same sort of artless beauty. He shook away this loss.

'Wanting sex is not a sin, Violet. You are a grown woman who has the licence to do exactly as she wills. And I want you as much as you want me.'

'Is it enough though, do you think, this want?'

'I've offered more and you declined it.'

'I declined it because lust is not a stable foundation stone for any marriage.'

'Who said it was only that?'

'Isn't it?'

He smiled. 'When you work out what you think this is let me know.'

'I'd like to be in bed with you right now. Where is your town house?'

'Close by.'

'And how hungry are you?'

'For food? Not at all hungry.'

His heart skipped a beat as she nodded and stood, placing the menu down on the unused setting. In a dream he called the waiter over, apologising for their sudden departure and placing a generous amount down on the table to allay any loss of business.

'After you, my lady.'

He was amazed they managed to get to the carriage without touching each other, but once inside he felt the full force of her want as she lifted his hand and took his forefinger into her mouth, her tongue laving along the side of it.

His other hand fell to her skirt and the outline of her thighs before climbing upwards.

'I want you naked in my bed. I want to lift your arms above your head and taste you and then…'

He stopped as she bit down on his hand.

'And then you will understand, Violet, that when you play with fire you should expect to be burned.'

'You promise?' The words were whispered, dangerous, breathless.

'Oh, but I do, my love, from the very bottom of my heart.'

He placed her palm across the erection straining against his breeches and she did not pull back but rather sat there feeling his shape. The streets of London passed by outside, the houses, the shops, the park, the people scurrying here and there. Ordinary happenings juxtaposed against what was inside, heat, breath and lust.

There was only a deep-seated need that he had never before felt with anyone in his life. He willed the town house on Portman Square into vision even as his heart sped into a rhythm that made him sweat.

An hour and a half later he wondered how he had lived without Violet. She lay beside him now asleep. Touching her lightly he watched her stir.

'You did not sleep, Aurelian?'

'I watched you instead.'

Her cheeks were flushed and her eyes unfocussed. The late sun slanted in the windows and he could hear all the normal daytime sounds outside.

'I have never wasted away an afternoon like this before,' she said.

'Wasted away may not be quite as I see it.'

'How do you see it?'

'Loved away.'

'Oh, I like that.'

Her hand stretched out and the signet ring he had given her glinted on her thumb. He was glad that she still wore it.

'Your town house is beautiful by the way. Has it been newly refurbished?'

'It is rented but I had it done at the same time as Compton Park, my home in Sussex.'

'So you might relocate to England?'

'I'd like to after all this is finished.'

'Then you will leave the game of intelligence?'

He nodded. 'It is something I should have done years ago. Shay and Celeste have been prompting me to make a decision, too.'

'What will you do there?'

'Become a farmer, I think. Ingratiate myself into the local community and have ten children.'

He felt her stiffen and wondered why, her face turned away from his.

'You did not have children with Harland?'

One tear splashed down on his chest, followed by another and when he tried to get her to look at him she wouldn't. 'I can't.' Her words were quiet. 'My husband had offspring with one of his mistresses but not with me.' She pushed herself away from him, the gap on the bed a lot wider than it looked and though he tried to stop her, she struggled away.

'It is why only this is left to me, this…lovemaking,

for I know what it is like to live a half-life with some-one who blames you for all that you cannot do.'

She scrambled from the bed before Lian could find the words to say anything, seizing her clothes and pull-ing them on, one hand swiping away the tears.

'There will be nothing left, don't you see that? Har-land tried to break me and he couldn't but you will and I can't let that happen because I couldn't stand it.' Pulling on the last of her clothes she turned to the door. 'I need to go home.'

Lian could see she was quite distraught and that any discourse now would be futile.

He had estates that needed tending and the inheri-tance of a title that was one of the loftiest in France. To abandon the hope of children, of lineage, of the future and of the past was a thing he had not con-templated. The coldness around his heart made him wince but he could not quite find the words to dis-miss her worry.

'This is not the end of our conversation, Violet. We shall speak again when we can both muster our thoughts.'

She nodded her head and pulled her cloak tighter around all the hotchpotch of her garments.

'I would rather go home alone.'

'Very well.'

When the butler came at his summons he asked him to have the carriage brought around. He was up dressing as she stood there uncertain in her si-lence and when he was ready he took her down. They barely spoke and Violet did not glance back at all as the conveyance began to move away, her posture stiff and her hands tight fists in her lap.

She stood in her room and looked around the chamber with eyes that were different from the ones she'd had before she'd left here at the noon hour.

She had told Aurelian her greatest fear and he had not shouted at her, had not despised her but had calmly said they would speak of it again when they had both gathered their thoughts. But she had seen the blank shocked hurt on his face and he was a man who usually hid any emotion with ease.

What did that mean? She closed her fingers around the ring he had given her and wished that she was a different woman, a happier one, less scared and more fertile. For him.

But she could not change. Harland had punished her for it but Aurelian merely looked sad.

That was the worst of it all. He was a good man who deserved more. Turning to the window she gazed out over the rooftops and at the cold grey sky. She was so sick of being frightened and of being not enough and a day that had started with such promise had run down into disaster.

Tomorrow she would be different. Tomorrow she would claim her life back again and visit the bookstore. Perhaps she might find some medical treatises on the subject of bearing children at Lackington's and glean some hope of one day conceiving a child. Perhaps, too, on reflection, she could speak with Aurelian without so much emotion and try and forge another pathway forward for them both.

Harland's battering of her self-confidence had been most effective. He'd jammed the portraits of the two children he'd had with a mistress in her face at every available opportunity and she had been mortified. The basic reasons for marrying and being a wife were beyond her and as their relationship became more and more embittered she almost understood his desperation for an heir. The social status of being a lord meant everything to him and to have his title pass into the hands of a far-flung relative with living sons was a hard pill to swallow.

She shook her head. If he had taken the care Aurelian had with her, she might have managed something but his hard and brutal lovemaking in the first few years of her marriage had left her stiff and dry, the feelings engendered ones of loathing and fury.

With Aurelian she had only felt the magic. She let out her breath and dashed a tear from her cheek. If she could provide Aurelian with an heir she would never ask for another thing in her life, she swore she would not.

'Please God,' she began, and tapered off. There were more pressing problems than her own in the world and if she could just relax her body might begin to soften and ripen.

She ran her hands across the flat of her stomach and whispered her words with fervour.

'Please, God, please help me. Please.'

* * *

Aurelian met Lytton Staines later that night at Whites, and was relieved to see the Earl of Thornton already well enough into his cups to make him easy company.

'You look browbeaten, Lian. Is the Lady Addington running you into the ground? I heard you were at Wakes today and that you left before even eating.' He raised his glass and drank deeply. 'Here's to beautiful red-headed women and their penchant for histrionics.'

Without meaning to, Aurelian laughed, but Lytton was not finished.

'To give Violet Addington her due it seems that everyone in society is enamoured of her. Half the men have pleaded for her hand in marriage and the other half are already married. Did you know that?'

This observation coming on the back of his own failed marriage proposal had Lian looking up quickly but he could see no true sign of any knowledge on Thornton's face. A mere conjecture and a remark that had been thrown off casually.

'You seem under the weather, Thorn. Was your recent Scottish sojourn unsuccessful?'

'Very' came the reply and for a moment Lian had the distinct impression that Thornton was not quite as drunk as he made out. 'I'm thirty-five next week. God, thirty-five. Where did all those years go to? If I don't find a bride soon and have children this will be all that is left of the Thornton line.' Long, thin fingers gestured to himself. 'Well, be damned if I will let that happen.'

'You are thinking of marrying, then? Who did you have in mind?'

'Anyone. The next woman who catches my eye and is passably attractive. I no longer require great beauty but I do want wide hips.'

Lian couldn't help smiling as he took a glass of brandy from the table before him. Thornton had ordered half a dozen so he didn't think he would miss this one.

Breathing out heavily, the melancholy of the day wrapped itself around him. He wanted to simply stand up and go and find Violet. He wanted her so desperately that he shook with it. He also knew that he couldn't.

Still, Lian felt Thornton was waiting for some sort of confidence and racking his brain he found something to say. 'Perhaps just living is the best anyone can hope for. Politics and the raw reality of life can take things away from you before you knew you wanted them.'

'That's deep, Lian, and tonight I only can deal with shallow. My sister is ill, deadly ill, for it seems she might not survive even another month. I found this out today. She is twenty-nine and a half and mortality is staring us all down a barrel.'

The truth of the words was shocking, the laughter from a nearby table unwanted and intrusive.

'The antics of a spoiled society lord doesn't hold as much appeal as it used to, Aurelian. I want to settle down, to be a better man.'

'Five glasses of strong brandy won't be helping that and it looks like you've had more before these turned up.'

Staines had the grace to look guilty. 'You were always the best of us all, Lian. The cleverest and the most…mysterious. Everything comes easily to you and yet lately I think that perhaps it has not. You've lost a portion of your third finger to some hideous accident and your face has been almost sliced in half. These things don't come from living the life of a landed and coddled *comte*.'

Thornton raised his glass, his smile perplexed. 'Shay was the hero of England and you…perhaps you are the anti-hero with your French heritage? Not that it worries me for I like you anyway but…' He stopped.

'But?'

'There are rumours you are in England for more than a holiday and Viscount Harland Addington had his enemies. Is this the reason you were at lunch with his widow?'

Lian swore under his breath. He had forgotten the way London held its gossip in such high regard. In Paris, too, there was the propensity for such tittle-tattle but it was less noticeable somehow. He decided to be honest.

'Violet Addington has nothing to do with why I am here. I simply enjoy her company.'

'Then let us drink to simple, Lian, and to hell with it all.'

Thornton went to raise a toast but his elbow slipped,

the brandy glass falling to shatter on the black and white tiles below, the frowns from those around directed their way.

'Come, I will take you home,' Lian said. 'Tomorrow the day might look brighter.'

But even as he said it he knew that it wouldn't. Lytton's sister was sick and Violet was barren, the future shrivelled into fragments that could not be put back together with a simple hope no matter how much one might want it.

The fine crystal crunched under his boots as they walked towards the door.

Chapter Nine

Violet knew she was in trouble as soon as she climbed
the stairs at Lackington's. She had asked her guard to
stay with the carriage, reasoning that a small allotted
time in the bookshop would not be a risky thing. She
had barely slept last night, the conversation with Aurelian running around in her head. Had she ruined
everything? She could not imagine life without him
there, his smile, his cleverness, his honesty.

She had seen the man about ten minutes after her
arrival at the bookshop, a thickset, swarthy gentleman who made no attempt at hiding his interest in
her. Leaving the less peopled section of the library
she made with haste for the busiest area of the room,
sitting with the pretence of reading her book, a rush
of panic sliding down her backbone when she saw
the man was still there. When he came over to her
she looked up.

'I have a pistol in my pocket and I need you to come
with me now.'

His words were quietly said but she could hear the

truth in them. Her eyes fell to his jacket pocket, the shape of something heavy there in the fold of cloth.

'If you do not, I shall shoot a person at random and their death shall be on your head. Do you understand? I am being well paid for this mission and I mean to complete it.'

His gaze took in a young mother on the far side of the room, two small children at her side.

Violet knew he meant what he said for she had spent enough years with her imbalanced husband to recognise another of the same ilk.

With care, she placed her book to one side and stood. When he gestured for her to go out through a small door at the back she could do little else. No one watched her leave. No one looked up as though things were not quite as they ought to be. The world of books and their patrons just carried on even as she was spirited out through the back and into a dark connecting passage. Then an arm came heavily around her and a pad of sweet-smelling cloth was applied to her nose. As she struggled, her limbs became heavy and numb and then all she knew was darkness.

Eli Tucker was waiting at the front gate of Lian's town house when his carriage arrived back in London just after six in the evening. The man looked furious and Lian's heartbeat skipped in his chest.

Violet. Something had happened to her.

Snatching open the door to the wind and the rain he leaped out.

'What the hell is wrong?'

'Lady Addington disappeared at Lackington's bookshop in Finsbury Square, sir, this afternoon around three. We were waiting out at the front with the carriage and when she did not reappear we went in to look for her. She was nowhere to be found and no one could remember seeing where she went. There one moment and gone the next. This was left on the seat of a chair in the main reading room.'

His gold signet ring sat in the palm of Tucker's hand.

'Someone has taken her.'

He should have stayed in London himself with the danger all around her and why the hell had she gone into the shop alone? He was furious at his own short-comings and that of his guards, the red roar of blood in his ears.

'Why didn't you damn well go in with her, Tucker? Everywhere is dangerous.'

'Lady Addington specifically asked me not to, my lord. She said she needed a moment of private read-ing.'

That sounded so like something Violet would say that Lian breathed in and tried to take stock of his fury. 'Take me to the bookshop now. There must be something we can find out.'

'I doubt anyone would be there at this time, my lord.'

'There will be a night watchman. He will have to do.' The fury in him mounted as he gestured for the guard to get in and commanded his driver to take him to Lackington's.

Twenty minutes later, Lian stood in the main room of the bookshop, a gas lamp in his hand as he looked at the chair his ring had been found upon. It was a good thirty feet from the main door but only five or so feet to a smaller door at the back. Whoever had taken Violet would not wish to garner attention, though Lian found it hard to believe she would neither yell nor scream as he forcibly kidnapped her. Yet another problem to think on. The skin on his arms puckered with fear and he shook such panic away, the cold of logic a far more reassuring emotion.

Striding through the now opened door into a passageway that was small and dark, he turned to the night watchman.

'Where does this lead?'

'The back entrance, sir. It is usually locked, though…' He petered out for plainly today it was not.

Peering at the ground, Lian hoped to see something, anything that could lead him to Violet. There were traces of a recent passing, the dust swirled in the sort of patterns that the hem of a passing skirt might make. Kneeling down, he shone the light closer.

'There.'

Footprints. Boots. Above a size eleven. Where were the corresponding ones of Violet's in the turned dirt further on? As he looked he came to the realisation there were none which meant she had been carried. Had her abductor used force to hurt her or to render her unconscious? Would it have been a blow to the head or the quieter use of some drug? He would stake his life on the latter. They wanted her alive, at least for a while, though the note she had shown him threatening death preyed on his mind.

Another door before them was also unlocked, a key and chain discarded on the ground outside. Lian picked them up and saw the cut through wide steel link. They had come prepared for the metal was thick and heavy.

'Where does this road lead to?'

'The main road, sir. It doubles around and then turns north.'

Everything was wet out here and he knew any clues that might once have been found would now be long gone. Still, he pulled at a broken twig in the hope of finding strands of red hair entwined about it. But there was nothing.

'You said she went missing around three?'

'Yes, my lord. The clock at the church had just struck the hour. I looked down to check on my own timepiece because it was running fast.'

'Then we will ride two hours from London and visit the inns. The dark would have been here by five at the latest and I have my doubts they'd have ventured further than that.'

Unless they had turned south or east or west? Or ridden on through the night?

He could not think about everything that might not be. He had to concentrate on what was likely. With sense and reason he would find Violet, he could only believe that.

They had stopped finally at a posting house, at least two hours having passed since they'd left the city. Her kidnapper had uttered barely a word for the whole journey leaving Violet to surmise that others would be there to meet them.

Her stomach felt sick with fear, the pad of sticky sweetness that had been held over her nose leaving her with a heavy head ever since she had awoken. Had Aurelian found the signet ring? Would he come to find her? Everything rested on him for she knew there was no other man in the world who could save her now. The tone of their last meetings also worried her for the closeness she had felt with him had dissipated somewhat under all the confessions between them.

The man in front leading her into the inn stopped. 'If you try to run I will use my gun, do you understand? I have nothing at all to lose by it now that we have come this far.'

She did not meet his glance as she nodded. With Harland any eye contact always annoyed him further and she did not want to risk the same here. What would they want with her? What could she tell them that would allow her more time?

Surprisingly once inside she was taken to a tidy room, the door closing behind her. Walking to the window she tried to open it but it was jammed tight with paint and age. One storey up. It would be possible to jump if she could only open it.

Taking her knife from her pocket she began to shave away the wood, rattling the window every second or so just to see if she had loosened it. The panes were too tiny to crawl through even if she could break them so she would have to pull the window itself free.

Forty minutes later, the key turned in the lock. Hiding her knife in a pocket she stood before the glass, hoping that the newcomer would not notice the pile of wood shavings on the sill and floor.

A different man entered and this one looked more dangerous than the last. He was older, larger and altogether angrier.

'Come.' He gestured to the door and she had no alternative but to follow him, down a passageway and then some stairs. At the end of another corridor was a tiny cell, solid iron at its entrance apart with a small grated peephole high up.

'There has been a change in plans and you are to stay here for the night.'

Swallowing, Violet looked into the gloomy dark as she heard the scurrying of tiny feet. The smell was of old hops and alcohol and fermenting straw. Further off were the louder voices of men.

When she did not step forward he grabbed her roughly, hitting her on the side of the head with his fist and shoving her in.

'Be quick about obeying instructions, my lady, or you will be dead.'

Did he know who she was or was he just being facetious? The pain of his blow had her falling to her knees, her arms wrapped around herself in order to fend off another punch.

Then the gate was shut and the light went with him, leaving her in a complete and utter darkness.

* * *

Aurelian reached the third tavern just after eleven. There was a carriage in the stables and five horses bedded down. Not a busy place, then, and largely off the road. He was thankful for the full moon which allowed them light.

The innkeeper was cagey and brusque when he answered the door.

'We have a large party coming so you would be better travelling on, sir. There's a posting house on your right three miles north which should be able to see to your needs.'

Lian looked up at the peeling façade and noticed a curtain twitching on the second floor.

'I'll go and try my luck there, then. Good evening to you.'

As he walked back to the carriage he signalled to Tucker to stay where he was inside and called out the new directions to his driver. Within a moment they were off and he made a point not to look back. He didn't want to give any impression that he knew things at the inn they'd just left were unusual.

'Things don't add up. I'm sure Lady Addington is there,' he said to Tucker as soon as the carriage began to move and the man beside him nodded.

'The mounts were not freshly ridden when I checked them over in the stables, my lord, and the carriage was unmarked. Strange there should only be the one conveyance, though, with the road being as busy as it is.'

'They are expecting others in the next few hours

from what I can gather. There were many clean glasses left at the bar when I glanced in and the fire was still banked.'

'They are waiting up, then?'

'I should imagine so.'

'Where is Lady Addington?'

'Only God and these ruffians know that for sure but we will pull in at the next bend and double back because instinct tells me she is there.'

He could not panic. Every decision he made from now on had to be well thought out. For Violet's sake. If he scared them they might just kill her and flee.

No one had followed them and for that he was grateful. Leaning out the window he called for the driver to pull well off the main road at the next opportunity. If the visitors were coming from the north he did not want to be seen, but he had the feeling they would travel up from London.

Tucker beside him took a pistol from his pocket and checked the piece. 'We are to expect trouble, then, my lord?'

Lian nodded. 'She is there somewhere. Hidden no doubt. I think there is a basement so if they are keeping her a prisoner that's probably the best place to do it.'

He tucked his own gun through his belt and slipped a long knife into the sheath in his boot.

'If we can do this quietly it will be better, but if we can't…'

He left the rest hanging.

He should have brought more men but it was stealth he needed and Tucker at his side was as good as they got. Once again he was grateful for Charles Mountford's advice.

A few moments later they were cutting through the fields behind the inn. There had not been dogs when he had walked up to the front door the first time and it still looked quiet, a few lights on upstairs and the bottom room fully lit.

Gesturing to Tucker to watch the movements from outside Lian crawled through the undergrowth and searched for a way to get in. Finding a window, he pried the fastening open and slipped through.

It was much darker here than outside. With his hands against the walls for direction, he walked on, the skitter of feet and the gleam of eyes to both his left and right. Rats. If they had put Violet down here…

He shook off fury and listened. The drip of water close by, the further call of a nightbird. Shallowing back his breath he tipped his head and heard it. A small sniff followed by another. He crept forward.

A man was asleep on a chair, a candle at the desk beside him. He dealt with him silently and grabbed the light.

'Violet?'

Whispered into the dark even as he rummaged through the pockets of the one lying down before him. No keys? A further glance noted a thick and solid cell door. He swore under his breath and looked through a tiny grate and she was there on the other side of the metal when he raised the candle to look, her face bruised and her eyes red.

'Aurelian?'

He made himself take a breath. 'I will have you out in a moment.' Already he'd found the wires he always travelled with, unravelling them from his pocket and bringing them up to the substantial lock.

The door opened before she could even say more, the stillness in him blended with the shadows, his hands sure and firm. His warmth and solidness wrapped about her fright, the candle he held flickering but staying alight.

'How many?'

'I have seen three.'

'Have they hurt you?'

'No.'

The bruise was smarting on her face though she forced down the tears as he asked his questions. He did not need a watering pot to distract him. It was dangerous here and these men were fully armed. She wanted to ask how he had found her and who was with him but he'd moved forward already out of the cell past a man on the floor who was either dead or unconscious. She did not want to look at him properly to know, but felt no sorrow for either state.

'Stay behind me.'

His ring glinted in the light as they passed a window. So he had found the signet ring at Lackington's and then come for her.

He moved like a big cat might, sure and fleet-footed, as though the semi-darkness was nothing. She wondered how many times he had done this, rescued someone needy from dire circumstances, killed a man and held a knife in his fist as though to welcome violence. Many, many times she imagined for the dangerous edges of him here were well on display.

Her fingers laced now into his own, and she relished the strength of him as he blew out the candle and discarded it.

'Thank you.' Her words came small and whispered and she thought he might bat them away until later but he did not.

'Thank me when we are safe, sweetheart.' His lips fastened across her own in a rapid surge of warmth and then let go, the cold reclaiming her.

Sweetheart. She held on to the word turning it over and over until all the translations were tangled.

'He loves me, he loves me not, he loves me, he loves me not.'

She recited these words as they walked towards a light at the far end of the corridor, part in fright and part in hope. There in the bowels of hell he was her heaven, a man who had risked his life to save her and was still risking it.

The footsteps above were louder, running now, clattering across the floorboards in haste, the shouted words of fury accompanying them. A voice she knew was there, too, her guard at the town house, Tucker.

Aurelian took a pistol from his belt swearing roundly in French as he raced up a set of stairs to one end of the room.

'If they come, you are to run. There is a wood behind the inn to the west. Go there. Stay low and hide. I will find you.'

'West?' Which direction was that. All her faculties were frozen in the fear of what he said.

Her own knife had been lost in the darkness when the man had hit her and she had nothing to help her rescuer with. Leaning over she picked up a heavy silver chalice from a table near the doorway, her fingers clawing around the missile.

This was all her fault. She could not run and leave him to deal with the mayhem, a man who had been sent to patch up the political rifts her husband's missing gold had caused between two nations.

Harland had always run. Away from responsibility, duty and obligation and any other thing that called him into account for his insatiable greed. Consequences and liability had meant nothing to him and his word was as full of holes as a sponge.

But here was another sort of man, one whose troths were given in integrity and honesty, one who might lose his life for the good instead of for the questionable. Fighting alongside a man like this would be an honour.

They came suddenly and without warning, three men with murder in their eyes and sharp blades. Aurelian pushed her over into a corner, hemmed in by a table on one side and a door on the other, his voice sounding nothing like it did a moment ago when he had spoken to her.

'Who do you work for?'

The man closest laughed, showing off a set of teeth that were missing many members. 'Those who ob-

ject to your interference in a matter that is a very
English one.'

'Cummings, then? And his department?'

The eyes of the other flared and then hardened.

'Did you know that your bitch here was the one
who started it all, the one who stole the first settle-
ment of gold?'

'I did.'

That brought on a slight shift in the room, an awareness that all was not quite as it seemed.

'I had also heard that some of the gold had been
changed into things that were easier to move. More
untraceable if you like.'

The silence allowed Aurelian to continue on.

'Sapphires. Rubies. Precious jewels.'

He was like an angler with fine bait on his line and
dangling it over a small pool containing hungry fish.

The first man bit. 'Where is it?'

'Kill Lady Addington and you will never know for
she has hidden it.'

'But you are a different matter. Your life will be
a pleasure to take and the master will be here soon.'

'Or he won't be?'

'Pardon?'

'Surely you do not think the one who pays you
would walk so blindly into a trap? You are surrounded
and he will know it. Men like him are too clever to be
implicated in the messy world of murder and treason.
Whereas you...' He tailed-off but he had caught their
attention now, Violet could tell that he had.

'You are the bait. You are the ones the law will deal

with while he gets away free though there is something you could do that might change it…'

'What?'

The man came closer, his knife momentarily lowered, and it was then that Aurelian struck. Without
mercy and with a speed that was unforgiving. The
first man lay at his feet as he reached for the second,
a hard slash across an unprotected throat. The third
man ran, the big one who had hit her, his cry cut off
even as he reached the doorway, a blade thrown across
the room to lodge deep into his lower back.

Silence echoed as pooling blood seeped into a tat-
tered rug. An owl outside called across the night.
Violet watched as Aurelian kneeled to each body,
emptying their pockets and removing their shoes to
search them before retrieving his knife.

'People like this always leave clues,' he said, tucking a sheet of paper away in his jacket.

'Will others come?'

'Perhaps and we don't want to be around when they
do.' He stood then and took her arm and she could see
the quick calculations for safety in his eyes.

'We will make for Essex. They won't expect that.
Addington Manor is just south of Colchester, is it not?'

'Yes? But there is nothing there…' She broke off.
'The list? You want it?'

'There are still things that don't make sense and
until I see the written list I can't be certain of who
is behind it.'

'You don't think it's Cummings?'

'Did you ever meet Antoinette Herbert? A French-woman who lives here in London?'

'The name is familiar.'

'Tall, blonde hair, with a mole just here.' He leaned over and touched the skin under her bottom lip just as a flash of recognition filtered through.

'She was at George Taylor's studio once. He was an artist and the woman was sitting for a portrait.'

'Was Harland present?'

'Yes.'

'I think she was his mistress until she became Cummings's.'

'That explains things a little bit. Amara said she witnessed a fight between her brother and Douglas Cummings.'

'A fight?'

'She heard her brother threaten him. They stopped though when they realised she was in hearing distance but she told me she felt that they were arguing over a woman.'

'I think Cummings is guilty of taking some of the gold but I don't think he is the one killing people. I think the list you found was one showing the hands in which the gold lies.'

'You went to see Cummings? When you were away?'

Lian nodded. 'I didn't see him but I saw his mother.'

Aurelian had left London to visit the Cummings country house. He thought Douglas Cummings would be there and wanted to meet him alone.

The manor was old and run-down and the maid

who had answered the door showed him through to a room after he gave her his card. An older woman was sitting in a wing chair with a knitted blanket tucked in across her knees.

'Comte de Beaumont? You are a friend of Douglas's? I am afraid he is not here today though I imagine I will see him tomorrow.'

'I am not sure *friend* is the right word, Mrs Cummings. I am here in a more official capacity.'

'Then he is in trouble. I told him all this would lead to no good, all his help and worry, but he felt it was his duty and so…' She petered off, dabbing at her eyes.

'Duty?'

'His sister. My daughter. This house. The servants. He has a good heart, but our well-being has taken up his whole life.'

'Is your daughter ill?'

'No, she is worse than that. She is simple and requires good attention so we have to hire two maids to see to her needs for she is too strong for me to manage any more. If my son has one failing it is that he is too concerned for others. I have told him that again and again but he will not listen and I wonder sometimes where he gets the sort of money needed to pay for it all.'

'Do you know the names Stephen Miller and George Taylor? Were they friends of your son's?'

Her eyes widened. 'He does not have many friends but I do remember him speaking of those two. I think they were jewellers, if memory serves me well.'

'It does and thank you.'

The fire was low and he crossed the room to add more wood, making certain the fire guard was in place as he finished.

Douglas Cummings's mother was old, his sister was sick and he had a property that was in need of urgent attention.

If Cummings had some of the gold, then there would be an element of blackmail in the mix, as well, for it would be easy to discover that he worked for the Home Office.

Antoinette Herbert had visited Stephen Miller in custody but had left before he had died. Had she administered some slow-releasing poison? The froth at his mouth could be explained by that. Perhaps she had administered it to stop him from confessing some fact that might implicate her?

Violet's voice brought him back from his thoughts.

'If anyone traces us to the inn and what happened there, will there not be questions?'

'I will protect you.'

'From the law of England?'

He smiled. 'Yes, even from that.'

She had worked out the implications so very quickly. He did not know at that second if that was a good thing or a bad one but what he did know is that he needed to get her away from everyone.

Cummings had probably taken the gold as a way out of debt and hardship but all instincts told Aurelian that he was not the killer. However, if he was wrong then Mountford could well be in on it, too. What had the Minister replied when he had asked him once if he trusted Cummings? With his life, he had said. Aurelian frowned. Well, it might indeed come to just that if he was not careful.

He'd seen the fear in Violet's eyes as she had looked at him after dealing with her kidnappers but he had got so used to allowing his enemies no leeway that he could no longer change himself.

He was who he was, the softness in him long since disappeared after years of being enmeshed in political intrigue. He was the end point of violence, the final adjudicator.

Shay had said that to him once in France as he'd helped him escape. He had also offered a warning.

'I did not care if I lived or died, Lian. When you reach that point there is a danger.'

Well, he could have said the same to Violet on the night she rescued him from the freezing street in Chelsea. He'd just killed again under the guise of politics, but he had held no true heart in the business.

Now he did, and protecting Violet from harm was as different as night and day to all that had come before. He could see the bruises on her face and arms in the light and he knew what the three men's intent had been for the note he had taken from the pocket of the man who had run confirmed everything.

'Rough her up if she becomes difficult. Kill her only as a last resort.'

He swallowed down bile and tried to contain the fury, but he was shaking with it and Violet's face did nothing to help that. Why would they not want her dead? Because she knew something or at least they perceived that she did. Her cheek was swelling and the mark under her left eye was darkening. He did not want to ask her of it, either, not now, not when he knew he still had not caught the main perpetrator and that the culprit was out there somewhere.

'It is my fault this has happened…'

He shook the words away. 'I would put the blame firmly on the greed of your husband.'

He sounded stern and he could not change that. They were miles from home, it was dark and he knew that whoever it was who had paid to kidnap Violet was coming north.

She nodded and swallowed away saying more, but he could tell she was not only frightened but disappointed. In him. In the killing. In the blood, violence and fury.

He hurried her away, his hand falling from her arm as soon as she was in the conveyance waiting on a side road within ten minutes walking distance from the tavern.

He turned to Tucker who was standing beside him.

'I need you to stay here and watch to see who it is who will arrive. If there is no one here still by the morning then take a carriage back to London and I will send instructions as to what I want you to do next.'

'Very well, my lord.'

'Don't let anyone see you. It will be a strong lead if we can identify the one who comes here.'

Violet frowned. How many times could Aurelian de la Tomber save her from death? When did he become tired of killing men to see her safe? The hours when they had lain together breathing each other in seemed distant for the spaces between them now lay in lives and lies and danger.

She began to shake unexpectedly, small shivers at first and then large tremors that overtook everything. Her very existence had become one of enormous highs and dreadful lows, a mix of fear and hope and desperate need.

She saw Aurelian watching her from across the carriage. He had not sought the place next to her but sat instead opposite her.

'I will not let them hurt you.' Formal words with little emotion or connection. She screwed her hands into the fabric of her skirt and held her fingers tight.

His whole demeanour was stiff, the pistol held across his lap as he scanned the road outside. He was expecting the others, she supposed, the ones the man had spoken of, though inside the inn he had implied they would not be coming.

Scaremongering, she imagined, and intimidation. When nothing seemed quite as it ought there was a far greater propensity for chaos. Constant shivering made her feel sick to the stomach, a lack of any food and water overlaying that. But this was not the time to admit weakness and so she sat up straighter and willed her fears back into the box that they had escaped from. A sudden tiredness came over her, the lack of sleep catching her unawares and she closed her eyes for a moment to rest them.

She awoke as the carriage stopped at a small tavern screened by a row of trees.

'Where are we?'

Aurelian was sitting close beside her now, his shoulder had been her pillow, the linen in his shirt creased from her sleep.

'We have made a slight detour and the driver is enquiring about horses for us to use before he goes on with the carriage to London. We will head out on a different road after I find you clothes that are more comfortable and less…feminine.'

'A disguise?'

'It would be best.'

'It is dangerous?'

'No. It's more that I do not want others to remember us and talk. Addington Manor is a day and a half's ride away from here and we will camp in the woods on the way.'

Within an hour they were ready, her new clothes unfamiliar but comfortable. She was no longer a lady but a youth, a groom who rode beside his master, a man of business on their journey to Essex.

She was amazed at how easily Aurelian had procured all the items needed. With very little fuss he had found sleeping mats and blankets, a pot, two knives and pewter cups to tie on the saddle of the horses he had bought, the coinage he had handed across to the tavern master substantial.

He was wearing the clothes of a trader or a traveller and she smiled at the comparison. Whatever he wore suited him, the rougher spun fabrics and oldness of his garments lending him another charm.

She imagined what it might be like without the pressures of society upon them, simple travellers wending their way through the countryside on a humble quest. The thought was beguiling, to disappear from all that she was and to have Aurelian beside her.

How much her life had changed in the last few weeks and if the danger of it still tracked them at least this side journey to Addington Manor offered a small respite.

Aurelian looked over at Violet as they made their way east. He was glad for the promise of a quiet and uninterrupted time. The danger of everything was lessened in this change of direction for no one would be looking for them here.

Violet was a proficient rider, her legs guiding the roan mare easily, and the morning sky was clear of rain. He could barely remember a time when he had felt so free of worry, the fear of losing her melting into the joy of reunion.

'When did you learn to ride?'

'When I was a young girl, Papa was adamant I should have a good seat. After I married Harland, though, I seldom got on a horse so this is exhilarating.'

When she laughed her eyes sparkled and the red tail of her hair beneath the hat caught the light.

'Yesterday I was sure that I would die, Aurelian, and yet today…' She shook her head. 'I can't believe we are here, on horseback, together and safe.'

He liked the joy in her voice. 'Wait till tonight when we sleep under the stars. Do you know the constellations?'

'No.'

'Then you are in for a lesson, and a good one at that.'

She laughed again. 'I used to wonder what it would be like to feel as truly happy as I do now. I wish we could have met years ago when I was young.'

'How old are you?' His voice was full of humour.

'Twenty-seven.' She grimaced.

'Ah, so very ancient. How old were you when you married Harland?'

'Twenty. Just. It seems like a century ago.'

'There should be a mandate,' he replied. 'Marriage ceremonies can only be performed for those above the age of twenty-five.'

'I'd sign that. Who can truly know their mind when they are so young?'

'Do you know it now, Violet?'

She blushed and he leaned over to take her hand. It was small and warm and her fingers folded into his own.

Hours later the dusk was upon them and Aurelian dismounted and motioned to her to do the same.

'We will walk from here. There is a river close by and the trees will shelter us from any notice.'

She did as he asked and followed him in, pushing the bare tree limbs aside and grateful for the other greener bushes that dotted their pathway. Fifteen minutes later he stopped and tied his horse to a tree, removing the saddle with a quick and easy movement before walking over to her.

The shadows made it all colder and although there was no snow on the ground it was freezing.

'I'll have the fire going in a few moments,' Lian said, dealing with her saddle in exactly the same way as he had his own.

Stretching, she tried to get the cricks from her back. It had been years since she had ridden so far and she felt the pain of muscles she had not used in a very long while.

Still, as he laid out their bedding and looked around for wood to light a fire she made herself do the same, collecting an armful of dry sticks in a matter of moments.

When she placed them down near him and he gave her a blanket she took it gratefully, tying the wool around her shoulders.

'You have done this many times?'

His eyes were laughing as he looked up. 'I have.'

'I suppose self-sufficiency is a mandatory character trait for a spy?'

'That it is.' His hands were busy now with a small piece of wood as he turned a twig on its surface with a length of thin thread. Within a few seconds flame flared and, adding other twigs, he soon had a fire, a man at home in his world and in everything that it threw at him.

The hesitancy between them was apparent. Her barrenness was only a part of a larger problem for he was the heir to the Dukedom of Lorraine-Lillebonne, a noble family whose lineage stretched across generations.

Granted he was also modern thinking but every man wanted the chance of immortality, progeny stretching into the future and making some sense of what was and what had been. Aurelian de la Tomber would be no exception despite any protestation he might give to say otherwise. She wished she was different, younger, more innocent, more able to be the woman he needed.

Their clearing was sheltered from the wind but she could hear it in the trees above them, whining. With the heat from the fire and the blanket he'd given her Violet felt almost warm. And drowsy, too. It was the fright she supposed from all that had happened, a fragility that made her bones weak.

'Is it safe here, Aurelian? Will anyone have followed us?'

'No. I promise it.'

'The law has a far reach though?'

'And we are on the right side of its jurisdiction.'

'But for how long? If Cummings is involved he will find a way to blame us for the deaths of those at the inn.'

'The man outside your cell was a known felon. I recognised his name and he had papers in his pocket that cannot be ignored.'

'Papers?'

'A docket for the payment of twenty guineas. An order for his services in your kidnap perhaps? We might be able to trace that.'

'Was there a signature?'

'No, unfortunately. The second man was French and the third one had this in his breast pocket.'

Aurelian placed a charm wrought in gold on her palm. 'Do you recognise it?'

She knew this piece of jewellery immediately for it was the same as the one she kept hidden in the crack of her floorboards. The shock of it made her stand. 'I do. It is a part of a necklace, a lost segment. I have another piece at home almost identical.'

His own interest was apparent. 'Where did you find it?'

'In Harland's library at Addington Manor. He had been arguing with a woman and when they left I found a sapphire and four gold segments of chain beneath his table.'

'Do you know who the woman was?'

She felt anger surge. 'He had many liaisons after... he began to dislike me. I never saw her though and I don't know her name.'

'Do you remember anything of her voice?'

Violet shook her head. 'I was upstairs and the door to his library was closed. It was the tone of the words I remember most clearly.'

'The tone?'

'Anger. Fury. All those things he used to be with me. If the sapphire is indeed a part of a necklace then it could be found. Jewellers tend to note such valuable articles and if we are careful we may be able to trace it.'

'I will put out the word.'

'Could it have been the jewellery of the one you

spoke of? The Frenchwoman who you saw leave Cummings's house?'

Aurelian laughed then. 'You sound just like Shay. A sleuth in the making.'

'I will take that as a compliment.'

'It is.'

And just like that the feeling between them changed, the air becoming thinner and the skin on her arms rising into need. The power of sensuality surprised her.

He felt it, too, she could see he did, for his gold eyes flared as he stood, bringing her in to him, his fingers on her cheek where she had been hit and his voice hoarse.

'Does it hurt?'

'No.'

'If it had been worse...'

'It wasn't.'

His mouth came down across hers, warm and tender with the underlying flavour of a wildness tempered and she met him halfway with her own need, unhidden and primal. An equal taking and giving, a touch that was wanted and returned, her insides melting into heat.

They were a part of the scenery around them, melded into the greenery and the silence as they lay down, alive completely, even in the winter cold. The bed made from brush and blankets was surprisingly comfortable and as the light faded into darkness the lines all around them blurred into charcoal. Aurelian pulled the thick blankets up so that only their heads were visible as she clung on to his warmth and strength.

Above them the stars were strewn across an endless sky, quick bursts of cloud cover only fleeting. The beauty of the wide open enormity of the heavens was something that Violet had seldom given much thought to before. She'd always had walls around her and barriers. Here the freedom brought tears to her eyes.

'They drugged me when they took me from Lackington's. I think it was laudanum, sweet smelling and fast acting.'

'Yes, probably laudanum.'

'Have you ever used it?'

She felt rather than saw him smile. 'To kidnap someone? No.'

'How did you know they had taken me? Who found the ring?'

'Tucker. He was waiting for me when I got back to London.'

'But to find that particular inn on the road among all the others...?'

'I guessed.'

'Then you must be good at guessing, Comte de Beaumont.'

Again, he smiled. 'Oh, I am, Lady Addington. I am good at other things, too.'

She moved towards him, face-to-face and pressing in. 'What sort of other things?'

His hand unbuttoned the fall of his breeches and he pushed them down. 'Loving you. Wanting you. Needing you.'

'Now?'

'All day while we were riding. All the hours of searching for you, too. Nothing can stop it.'

'Even my inability to bear children?'

He turned her beneath him and positioned himself to enter her. 'Least of all that.'

Then they were joined, heat rising in the cold, a gasp of breath, the race of blood, heartbeats gathered into a single rhythm. She cried out and the sound echoed back to them in the hollowed glade, over and over, the sweet release that took her making everything right again.

It was morning when she opened her eyes, Aurelian was nowhere to be seen. The birdsong was prolific and shrill and the hundreds of small insects awakening to the new day twirled and zinged in the breaking arcs of sunrise.

Stretching, she felt reborn and it delighted her, the dry and brittle woman she had been for all six years of her marriage softened now and receptive. She liked the scent of him and the feel of him and the taste.

This was how God had made people, she then thought, all her senses startled into notice, every fibre of her being wanting him.

He returned after a good quarter of an hour, three fish dangling from one hand, a man at home anywhere and well able to provide for himself.

'You look like Poseidon home from the sea.'

'Come to seduce a nymph with fish?'

'If you can provide me with breakfast I think I shall succumb.'

'Give me a moment, then.'

He started a fire with the same ease as he had yesterday and proceeded to fillet the fish he had caught.

'What are they?'

'Two bream and a perch. Napoleon does not send money to feed his troops as they cross the lands they vanquish. One has to improvise or starve.'

He had starved often, Lian thought then, the humour of the day wilting. In the north of Spain and in Portugal and in the cold of the Pyrenees. But he had been lucky, too, for many others had not survived to tell the tale.

Banishing such maudlin reflections, he reasoned that for this moment no one was near enough to be dangerous to them or a threat of any kind. It was just himself and Violet, the hat she had worn yesterday discarded this morning, the length of crimson settling across her shoulders and down her back.

The bruises on her cheek were darker, the puffiness under one eye spreading. A battered beauty but brave. He could barely stop himself from putting the fish to one side and finding her warmth.

But she looked both tired and hungry and they hadn't eaten much since yesterday morning. They would reach Addington Manor some time in the afternoon and needed sustenance to see them on their way.

'You were up early?'

'I sleep better with you than I ever do alone.'

He gave her these words because the truth in them was startling. He could not remember a morning in years when he had awoken so late to the sound of birdsong.

'It is the same with me. Perhaps we wear each other out.'

He laughed at that as he laid the first fillet of perch in to his small pan.

'Then I shall feed you to replenish your energy, my lady.'

'"If music be the food of love, play on."' She remembered the quote from boarding school.

'You read Shakespeare?' He asked this after a moment or two.

'Books were like friends to me when I had none.'

He'd liked to have met Harland Addington in life, Lian thought then, if only to place his hands about his throat and squeeze the breath from him.

He almost said as much but then decided against it given the mystery of the Viscount's death, which she had yet to explain. Pulling the fish from the pan, he served it on a plate taken from his saddlebag and watched as she lifted the white flesh to her mouth.

'Salt might have made it better, and butter, but...'

She shook her head. 'It is delicious, Aurelian. The most delicious fish I have ever eaten in my life. Thank you.'

She was not a woman to stand on ceremony. That thought warmed him considerably, for how often had he been in the company of females who did not appreciate the simple things?

His mother had been the same, finding joy in humble treats and making the most of chance and change.

'One day I shall catch you a brown trout at Compton Park, for to me it is the king of all fish.'

'Compton Park is your house?'

'In Sussex. An hour away from Shay and Celeste's estate. It was a part of the reason I wanted to come to live in England.'

'I have heard stories of the beauty of it.'

'Yet to me it's simply home.'

'A place to stay, to settle.'

There was a puzzlement in her words that he wondered about and yet after his dismissed marriage proposal he had no desire to mention his hopes again.

Now was enough. This moment under this sky with fresh food to eat and good company to enjoy. Even the cold seemed lessened today.

He'd always been someone who looked ahead. But now with Violet he only thought of stopping which was just another way that she had changed him.

'I need to return to Paris to finish a few things and then I will be back.'

'The gold?' she asked and he nodded.

'Nothing is easy until it is finished.'

Chapter Ten

They reached Addington Manor by sunset and re-
trieved the list buried in the wooden box she had
placed it in. What could have been a difficult task
became easy as the family who had purchased the
property were abroad and the main servant who had
been left in charge was more than happy to allow Aurelian the time and space to find what he needed in
the outside gardens on the strength of a heavy purse
of coinage.

After leaving the manor they stopped in a copse of
woods a good hour south and Aurelian allowed her
the first opening of the box.

The list was still wrapped in cloth, a few dried
flowers alongside it. Violet took it out carefully and
unravelled the sheet of paper looking to see if what she
remembered on the note was still there before hand-
ing it to Aurelian for a closer look.

His finger traced the initials.

"'Stephen Miller" and "George Taylor". "Douglas

Cummings" is here, too, as well as "A.W.". Alexander Whitely. "J.C." is a question, as is the letter "A".'

Violet looked at him, frowning.

'It could belong to Antoinette Herbert, his French mistress. She was one of the last people to see Stephen Miller alive. I went to visit her and she knew who I was.' He pushed his hair back with his free hand and spoke more softly. 'I knew her name, too, from Paris. She said she was one of the contributors of the French gold.'

'But you think she was more than that?'

'Much more. She gave and then she took. It was a way in to find the gold.'

'Is she blackmailing Cummings?'

'Into killing, you mean? No.' He shook his head. 'Perhaps not that. Cummings has a sick sister, an ageing mother and an estate that looks as though it is in the last stages of falling down. He also has, according to that same mother, a heart of gold. I was there the day you were taken when I should have stayed and watched that you were safe.'

'I am safe now, Aurelian. But why did you want to see the list, then? What could it tell you that I have not?'

'This.' His finger ran across a mark next to the initials of the letter *A*. 'Harland Addington rubbed something out.'

He turned the paper over and held it up to the fading sky.

'A cross was placed there, in capitals.'

'A kiss?'

'Or the first sign of his realising that Antoinette Herbert, his mistress, needed to be dealt with?'

'You think he might have tried?'

'The fight you mentioned and the broken necklace. Perhaps Antoinette Herbert also saw this list and needed a way to tear Harland Addington into pieces.'

'That makes sense.'

Lian looked pensive. 'Did your husband ever hurt your nephews?'

The world spun around Violet in a frightening and dizzy whirl and she was suddenly hurled back into the horrible years of her marriage.

Harland's tastes were strange to say the least and he could be more than violent when he drank. Laudanum was there too, the sweet and sticky smell of the drug clinging to everything.

After Michael and Simon had come to live at Addington Manor she remembered bruises that had often been on their arms or cheeks. She'd put them down to the boys' boisterous games. But had Harland been threatening them with his certain sort of brutality until Amaryllis had simply snapped?

'I think he may have…' But she could barely say the words, the shaking that had started as soon as Aurelian had mentioned her nephews now taking over everything. It explained so much. Why Amaryllis had killed her brother and why she had hated him just as much as Violet had. It would also explain why Michael and Simon were so withdrawn for boys their age. They had lost a beloved father and then been sent to live with a vicious and sadistic uncle, often journeying down to

London with their mother to the town house in which Harland mostly stayed. He would have had a freedom to hurt them that was astonishing and Violet knew he would have enjoyed it.

Her husband had deserved so much more than a simple blow from a hammer. The fury in her made her cry out even as she felt herself falling.

Aurelian laid Violet down carefully and covered her with the blankets, trying to quell the shaking and make her warm.

She was freezing, her lips blue with the cold and each finger curled in a hard fist against her palm.

He had heard rumours in London of Addington's aggression. Now he knew that she had experienced what he had prayed that she would not have and that the dreadful truths of her husband's cruelty were also her truths.

The bastard had destroyed her in so many ways that Lian could only wonder how she might have survived, her kindness still there even after all the horror. He held her hand and willed warmth and strength into her, glad when her eyelids finally fluttered and she came back to him.

'You knew what he was like? My husband?'

'I guessed. Was Amaryllis the one who killed him? Did you cover for her because of the boys?'

'Yes.'

'Because you understood that it was not only the gold that had ruined him but sheer malice?'

'I didn't know about my nephews but I had seen others…'

'Others?'

'Other women. In his bed. He taunted me with them and they did not always look…' She stopped, and re-grouped her bravery. 'Happy. I prayed to God so many times that he might die and if I had said something to Amaryllis I might have saved the boys and her from everything that happened afterwards.'

'You did anyway, Violet. You and Amaryllis dealt with him in the best way you could.'

'Only you would tell me that, Aurelian, and it helps, but how can you look at me and not hate all that I have been?'

'Easily,' he replied. He leaned over and took her hand and she held on, feeling both his goodness and his strength.

'It is over, Violet. All of it. Now we just have to expose Antoinette Herbert and Douglas Cummings and the others and then everything will be finished.'

His eyes flicked back to the list.

'Could anybody have known that Harland wrote this? That he kept lists like this?'

'Perhaps. He was a man who needed things written down. Always. It was something he just did.'

'Then maybe they think you have things that would implicate them if they got into the wrong hands. Has your town house ever been robbed?'

'Yes, when I first came to London and then again some weeks ago. Nothing was broken or taken but every room had been gone through.'

'Perhaps because I have been asking questions. When the man in the boarding house tried to kill me on Brompton Place he said a woman had sent him.'

'Antoinette Herbert?' There was a whisper in her words.

'I would bet money on the truth that she is the one and that the others on this list were her minions.'

Early in the afternoon they headed towards Sussex in a fast carriage Aurelian had rented.

Aurelian wanted to show Violet his life, his house, his past, all the losses and the gains. Safety also beckoned at Compton Park with its attending quiet, and with the men he had employed watching the perimeters they could stop and breathe and begin to understand each other in a way that would lead them forward.

He hoped that the opulence and beauty of his home would not frighten Violet but would heal some of her cracks as it had his own. He didn't want her to feel distanced by its wealth or its majesty.

Beside him Violet looked so much younger than she had even a week ago, her worry softened with the bruises on her cheeks largely faded. He could feel her breath against his arm.

He was glad his sister and aunts had left Sussex to go to their house just outside London and would not be visiting Compton Park again until the beginning of March. Leaning back, he closed his eyes for a moment, the tension of past three days having left him with a building headache. For all that was difficult, Violet was with him, her warmth comforting, her trust gratifying.

It would have to be enough for now until he could sit without interruption and in safety and be honest. There were so many things he needed to say to Violet and he could see in her eyes that she felt the same.

Compton Park was the most imposing house she had ever had the pleasure of viewing, its symmetrical three-storeyed façade boasting a great number of turrets and gables and parapets. The windows were numerous and mullioned, the glass panels glinting even in the dull sun of a February day.

The staff were all lined up in the bottom hallway, obviously having realised it was their master who had come home.

'You do not come here often,' she said to him before he stepped forward to shake the first man's hand.

'Rarely. My work has kept me in Europe.'

She could not even imagine leaving a house like this to go anywhere. The gardens were fully formed and the manor sat on a rise looking across a lake and down a long vista of trees and water features stretching into the far distance. The furniture held a French influence, the light lines and elegance of everything so un-English. The colours were different from most of the London town houses she had been in. There were light creams and yellows and a startling blue in the hallway, the more usual wintery mustiness of English interiors nowhere in evidence here.

Aurelian introduced her to the servants and they

bobbed down before her, and then finally they were alone in a smaller room at the back of the house.

'Mrs Hutchinson will show you to your chamber.'

'Will you be somewhere close by?'

'My room is next to yours. There is a connecting entrance.'

'And it is safe here?'

'Very. Come, I will show you.'

But the door flew open even as he gave his reply and a woman stood there. A beautiful woman with chestnut hair. Deep dimples graced both her cheeks and her hair roughly pulled back was escaping in untidy tendrils. She was also pregnant.

'Celeste?'

Aurelian began to smile.

'Summer is behind me.' She turned to look for him, the light catching the colour of her eyes.

'Violet, may I introduce Celeste Shayborne to you? She is Summerley Shayborne's wife and also a good friend of mine. Celeste, this is Violet Addington—'

'Oh, we're old friends already,' Celeste interrupted.

When Celeste smiled Violet was entranced.

'We heard you had been seen coming south. Summer felt you might be in danger so we brought a few of the tougher-looking servants with us.'

Her English was tinged with an accent and when she removed her gloves, Violet saw stripes of white scarring on one wrist that she'd not noticed the other times she had met Celeste. Her eyes then fastened on Violet's cheek.

'Someone has hit you?'

'Who has hit her?'

Summerley Shayborne now stood in the space behind his wife, his glance taking in the bruises on Violet's face.

'Violet was kidnapped and Douglas Cummings is involved somehow.' Aurelian answered the question.

'Where is Cummings now?'

'In London probably and trying to make a case against me for sending all his plans awry. I think he is being blackmailed by the woman behind all this.'

'A woman? Complicated?' Shay said this.

'Very.'

'Being French is not an easy thing in a country fixated on the danger of Napoleon Bonaparte.' Celeste joined in now and Violet saw in her logic a new peril.

'I can vouch for Aurelian's actions. He was with me.'

Even as she said this she understood another truth. Both she and Aurelian were in danger. She could see that everyone else in the room had understood this before she had.

Usually she was not so slow but she was exhausted and aching and the house here had folded its strength about her and made her falter.

'We have Charles Mountford on our side,' Aurelian said. 'I have discovered nothing that says he is in on it.'

'What of Violet, though?' Shayborne's query was sharp. 'If we know that she is here then others undoubtedly will. It could ruin her.'

'I am an ageing widow, my lord, who has already

been…*ruined* as you put it. Among his other failings, my dead husband was a man of greed and avarice and when this is known publicly, which it soon must be, I doubt I shall be on anyone's list of exalted guests. Frankly, it will be a relief.'

Celeste began to laugh. 'We live well enough away from Society and all its pretensions. But still, the choice of respectability is a wise thing to maintain if it can be managed.'

'I have offered Violet marriage to make our situation legal.'

Aurelian's words created a sudden silence, the mouths of both Summerley and Celeste Shayborne opening with astonishment.

'I am not a good proposition for your future. I have told you that.' She whispered her words fiercely, thinking of all that had transpired over the past few days.

'Violet cannot have children.'

This honesty brought the blood to her cheeks. 'I am certain that your friends do not wish to hear any of this.'

'Oh, but we do.' Celeste poured three drinks and proceeded to hand them around. 'A conversation like this demands fortification. You could definitely do worse in the husband stakes, Lady Addington. I have it on good authority there would be many others who would jump at the chance of being the bride of the Comte de Beaumont.'

'Enough, Celeste.' This came from Summerley.

Aurelian's hand wound into Violet's and she was

glad for the touch, though in the conversation she had felt no judgement. Perhaps there were groups of people that were simply honest with each other and who loved each other enough to be so. Strong people who did not care for the petty rules so prevalent in society and who did not judge people for faults or impediments or for rumour.

As Summer and Aurelian began to talk together, Celeste leaned over and asked her own quiet questions.

'Do you have family, Violet?'

'I don't. My parents died years ago and apart from a sister-in-law and two nephews I am alone.'

'Aurelian needs to settle in England. Here. In Sussex.'

'You are French?'

'My father was. I am the one who gave Lian the scar on his face. In my defence, I was trying to protect him and although he sacrificed a little vanity he kept his life.'

'You were a spy, too?'

'In Paris, but that's not something I tell many people.'

'Then I am honoured at such a confidence.'

'You have your secrets, too. Sometimes when they are held tightly they can only harm you and stop you from moving onwards.'

God, Violet thought, no wonder Aurelian and these people were good friends. They all had that knack of turning the world upside down, her years of carefully protected privacy washed away in minutes. And yet in their dismissal of her concerns they became lessened. Her barrenness. Her past. Her dreadful first marriage.

'You have lovely friends.'

She said this to Aurelian as she watched Celeste and Summerley depart, their time together a welcome break from all the fear of the past days.

'They like you, too. I haven't yet met a person, Violet, who hasn't fallen under your spell.'

'Harland didn't.'

'He was a fool. But for now you need to sleep. You are dead on your feet.'

'Your chamber is the one next door to mine?' she asked for confirmation again.

'It is.'

He did not offer more as he took her arm and walked with her, the staircase wide and beautiful as everything else was in the house. She was almost dizzy with fatigue and yet still she would have come into his arms on the tiniest of hints, mesmerised by a man who was as clever as he was kind.

At the doorway of her room, he kissed her forehead and delivered her into the competent hands of two maids who had supplied a bath of steaming water.

Much later she awoke to the darkness and the silence and the hugeness of an unknown room. For a moment she stiffened, panic beginning to fill her mind. The lateness of the hour was apparent and she heard the soft rap of a branch against her window.

Had she cried out? Had Aurelian heard her? The

house was still and so she lay there, too, watching shadows and remembering.

An hour later she was still not asleep and any repose seemed further away than it had been when first she'd awoken. With care, she sat on the bed and shifted her legs to the side, standing so as not to make any noise at all as she walked.

The world before her outside the window was blanketed in snow, a white wonderland of trees and hills and gardens and there was a peace here that was exhilarating.

A footfall to one side had her turning and Aurelian stood close. He had removed his neckcloth, his shirt falling away from the top of his chest.

'I heard you had wakened.'

'I tried to be as quiet as I could.'

He looked down. 'There is no silence in a house like this one.'

'You were not asleep?'

He did not answer this as he came to stand directly beside her, observing the landscape just as she was.

'In France my family has land they have owned for centuries, old land where our ancestors walk as ghosts. Moving to England allows me a new canvas to fill with my own memories.'

She liked that thought.

'Beginnings,' she whispered just as his voice came again across the darkness.

'"Remember tonight, for it is the beginning of always."'

'That's beautiful. Who said it?'

'Dante Alighieri, an Italian poet of the late Middle Ages.'

'You are a spy who quotes poetry and a man who can kill without a second thought. Who are you really, Aurelian de la Tomber, for I cannot quite fathom the truth of you.'

He turned to face her, sadness in his eyes.

'When you picked me up off that road, the snow swirling in the cold, I had almost given up on living. I thought you were an angel then, with your red hair against white skin and a voice that was…kind.'

'A fallen angel, perhaps.'

'Promise me something, Violet. Promise that you will discuss anything you are not happy about, anything that worries you.'

'I don't like sleeping in here alone.'

'Will you come with me to my chamber, then?' He offered her his hand, palm up and she took it.

His bedroom through the small door was enormous, one end filled with books and maps and ancient manuscripts.

'I had them brought over from Paris,' he said when he saw her looking. 'I have not had much time for reading but I mean to make some here.'

'And the piano?'

'It was my mother's.'

There were paintings on the walls that showed landscapes, foreign shores with a sun in the skies a lot warmer than the one here in England. On a desk near the fireplace was a bower of candles. A gun lay at an angle next to that.

'You expect more trouble? This is why you do not sleep?'

'I have guards placed from one end of Compton Park to the other. If trouble comes I will know about it well before it reaches our front door.'

'And you will deal with it?'

'Easily.'

She laughed. 'It must be so satisfying to believe in yourself like you do.'

'Don't you?'

She couldn't answer. As a child she had lost her mother, and then her father and stepmother had not wished for her company. Lately, though, after the hard years with Harland, she had been starting to regain something of herself, an independence and bravery, but even that was difficult. 'It's hard to be brave when you are so afraid.'

'And yet you stopped your carriage to pick me up?'

'Perhaps there is an end-point in fear, then. A place where you turn back into life because there is nowhere else left to go.'

'Or perhaps you were always a lot more courageous than you thought you were. You are shivering.'

He brought her against him, his warmth seeping through her coldness, the demons and ghosts of the past shifting from the light into the shadows. 'Come, let us get warm again.'

Always with him there was a sort of magic in touch, a connection that startled her. She felt it now in the promise of what might come next.

The bed was an old one with embroidered hangings on each side sporting images of deer and lions and horses entwined in bowers of ivy. He had removed his boots and his breeches followed.

His skin was so much darker than her own, the contrast making her smile, though when his hand came to cup her breast she was consumed by another feeling altogether.

Breathlessness. And anticipation. Her body rose up to meet his.

She was so damn responsive, nipples hardened and her arms around his neck bringing him in. There were freckles on her chest and her arms, a smattering of darkness on skin so pale he could see the blue blood lines upon it.

Differences.

The want in him built and breached like waves inside, a need that was so foreign it made him disorientated, the cool controlled world he'd always lived in shattered into pieces and falling to his feet like snowflakes.

Drifting.

If he lost her…

His finger came up to the mark under her eye, the dark bruise lighter now.

'Je te veux plus que je ne veux la vie elle-même.'

The words were said before he knew it and he wondered if she had any fluency in his language. He seldom spoke during lovemaking and rarely used French while in England, but Violet took away logic and replaced it with a desire that came from within and unbidden.

God, he was becoming a man he hardly recognised and she most certainly had never given him any troth of permanence. She'd refused his offer of marriage, after all, and insisted only on lust.

His mouth came down more roughly than he meant given his recent thoughts and he made himself slow down. She had been honest with him and that was all that he could ask. Now he needed to be honest, too.

He felt her breath hitch as he stroked her and understood that in lust there also lay pathways to something more. Her fingers dug into his back and he revelled in the pain of them for a slack response would allow him nothing.

Bringing her under him he came in with intent, no question in what he wanted, what they both wanted, the intimacy cleaving them as one. The past and the future disappeared as their blood beat in unison, cancelling out all that they lost when alone.

Faith, he thought, and tried to find the edge of something else, as well. Truth was there, as was relief. Relief that he should have had the luck to be found by a woman who completed him.

He broke away after their release, lying on his back and looking up at the ceiling laced in shadow. He could no longer pretend that she was only a companion in the pleasures of the flesh. It seemed wrong and belittling in the face of all that was unsaid.

'I want you more than I want life itself.' Her voice came through the silence, a word for word translation of what he had said before.

'You speak French?'

'Fluently.'

He began to laugh because here was a joy he had never felt in a woman's bed before. Gratitude and contentment and surprise.

'When did you learn?'

'At boarding school. My father found an institute for me that was well regarded and singularly academic. I can hold a conversation in Spanish and German, as well.'

'That does not surprise me.'

This time the laughter was her own.

'Why not?'

'Because you are unlike any other female I have ever known and I mean that as a compliment. Your intellect is a part of that.'

'Harland hated it that a woman could think.'

'Because he could not himself?'

She was still, her eyes misty and sad. 'I wish you had seen me then, before…' She stopped. 'Before I lost my way in life.'

'Have you found it again?'

Sitting up, she kissed his mouth in a fashion that made his blood run hot.

'I have.'

'Good. Then fight for your truths, Violet, and don't let anyone tell you different.'

He kissed the tip of her nose and stood. 'Get back into bed and I will go down to find us something to eat.'

She could not remember feeling so happy in all her years. Perhaps at school she'd had some moments of things seeming easy and interesting, as if there was a whole world out there just waiting for discovery.

But now Amaryllis and the children were safe, she was in a home well-guarded and secure, and Aurelian was beside her.

She wanted time to stop right now, to freeze into this second.

She wanted him to think that she was honourable and wise and clever and all the other things she had tried her hardest to become.

I want you more than I want life itself.

How had he meant that?

Want in the sense of carnal desire or want in the way of a yearning and permanent need?

Celeste Shayborne had said something in the same vein when she had spoken to her quietly after her husband and Aurelian had needed to find something in the library.

'The Comte is a man who has had many others depending on him in his life. He has always been a chameleon and a warrior as well as a dweller, too, in the darker places of the world, but he needs to settle down now, to be at peace with all that he has been and done. I think you of all people will understand that for you remind me of myself.'

Violet could not in all the world imagine any similarities. Celeste Shayborne had worked in intelligence in Paris but here in England she looked to be the perfect lady. The dingy secrets of her past with Harland were nothing to be proud of but there was a second as Celeste had spoken that Violet had felt a vivid and startling connection. It was as if her shadows were known and understood.

She shook her head. Such fancy and whims were like castles in Spain.

Aurelian was back with a platter of food even as she thought this, wine was there, too, a red she did not recognise and to one side lay a small bowl of marzipan sweets.

'From the Yuletide,' he explained when he saw her looking.

To have a man bring her food in bed was a glorious treat and she sat up fully as he laid down a napkin under the large pottery plate.

'I brought my chef from Paris when I came the first time and he liked the countryside here so much that he stayed.'

'The servants are French, too, then?'

'Only some of them.'

'Celeste is a very proper lady.'

The laugh took her aback.

'When she knows you better she may tell you the whole of her story. Everybody has a past, Violet, as much as they might not want to admit it.'

This was so close to what she had just been thinking that she blushed.

'Yours is attached to the legitimacy that intelligence affords. A slate that can be wiped clean again and again by the interests of state and crown.'

'There are always shades in such an occupation and the dark hues are more prevalent than you might think.'

'Was it the case for you?'

'I have killed men, Violet. Many men. Some in the name of Emperor and country but most because of the less respectable pragmatism of war. If you were to question my morality with those I worked with in Paris, there would be a variety of answers. Some flattering and others not. It would depend on how closely they knew me.'

'Shayborne, then. What is it he would say?'

'That he would not want me as an enemy. That ruthlessness often rules me and that the brutal and hard-hearted business of espionage has burnt into my bones as callousness. It still burns,' he added, 'make no mistake of that.'

'Why do you say this?'

'Because there is never just one answer as to a person's motives. Once I was a man who believed that trying to do good was enough, but it wasn't.'

'What changed you?'

'I told you of Veronique.' He waited till she nodded. 'But mostly I think it was the death of my mother. She was killed by a faction that believed the de Beaumont aristocrats were greedy sycophants who deserved a lesson. After she died I delivered them a stronger message back and it went on from there. A moment of change. A decision that led to others. All of life is like that perhaps, an action, a reaction and then a consequence. The consequence of standing up for what you believe in.'

'And if you don't? If you didn't?'

'Then find the point in your past that you did. It is

surprising on reflection how many times the downfall is unchangeable and then all you can do is live with it, the shame and the loss, and hope that you have done enough for it to never happen again.'

'Is it something you might tell others…this thing that changes you? Is that a necessary thing, do you think, to recover?'

'No.' He said the word almost without thought, strong and certain. 'It is enough for you to know it and acknowledge the debt.'

Tears came into her eyes at the gift of his words and his finger softly wiped them away as they fell.

'Tomorrow is a new day to vanquish ghosts. Count on that.'

She saw his smile and the dash of humour in his eyes and was grateful. He knew enough of shadows to dispel them before they overcame you and made you weep for all that was gone. She had never met a man before who had understood that.

The Christmas marzipan ball he popped into her mouth was delicious.

The letter came the next day ordering Aurelian to present himself in London. He was to bring Lady Addington with him.

The signature was that of Douglas Cummings and Lian knew enough of legal summons to also know it could not be ignored. But he had other plans entirely and the rider who had brought the missive had not placed it in his hands personally.

He did not want to take Violet to London where she

would be in more danger. Cummings and Antoinette Herbert were his prime suspects but he was certain there were others, as well, and he needed to find out who else was there alongside them.

When he told Violet of his plans, her reaction was not at all the one he imagined.

'I want to go with you, Aurelian. I won't stay here by myself so if you do not agree to take me I will come anyway.'

'You've been hurt once by these people and Compton Park is a safe haven. If you would prefer, you could stay with Shay and Celeste at Luxford.'

'I spent six years being told what to do by Harland and before that I was the property of my father but I am free now and the bravery that you spoke of last night is a precious gift I never want to lose hold of again. If you take me with you I won't be sitting here and worrying and I promise to do everything you ask.'

'It may not be easy, Violet. I don't intend to just walk into their lair and give myself up.'

'I didn't think you would.'

'Mountford may not be the man we imagine him, either.'

'But if I can talk to him and tell him all that has happened to me he might think twice.'

'What was his relationship with your mother?'

'He loved her and when she asked him to be my godfather he was happy for the duty. I saw many of Harland's associates personally over the time he was tampering with the gold so I might be able to identify them, as well.'

'You didn't know any of the ones who kidnapped you.'

'Please, Aurelian. Please let me come.'

He looked at her and saw in her eyes the hope that might save her. Save them. If only he could keep her alive.

When she smiled he knew he was in trouble and when she crossed the room and stood on her tiptoes to kiss him hard on the mouth he knew he was in even more.

They left Sussex in the very early morning of the next day and with as little fanfare as they could manage. The first carriage had gone on ahead last evening with Eli Tucker and two of the guards.

It was a strategic decision. If anyone was watching Compton Park then they could split the opposition before they reached London. Lian had asked Shay if they could use the Luxford town house even as the others went on to Portman Square.

Keep them guessing was a mantra he had employed from the first but he knew he had to flush out all those who were responsible for Violet's kidnapping and he did not mean to do it kindly.

They would pay for their mistakes. A part of him hoped Mountford was not involved as he owed a debt to the man after his warning about Violet's being in danger in the park.

He had organised to have a groom sit with the driver as well as the safety of another guard at the back. There were two shotguns and a pistol within reach inside the carriage. It never paid to be under-prepared.

Violet looked tense and worried as they finally met the main road which at this time of the day was a busy one and for that Aurelian was grateful. Anyone meaning to waylay them would probably think twice with all the onlookers, though their daring at Lackington's had rattled him.

Shay was travelling up to give his thoughts to the commission and for that extra weapon in his armoury Aurelian was glad. Celeste had come to see him, too, quietly impressing upon him the importance of protecting Violet.

'She is scared, Aurelian, and lonely but she is also brave. If you know what is good for you, you will not let her slip through your fingers and any woman should have the benefit of doubt in refusing a marriage proposal once.'

'You are an unlikely champion for Violet, Celeste.'

'I think she has as many demons as I had before I married Summer but she needs to understand that a good man can heal a chequered past. Did she kill the husband?'

'No, but she is protecting the one who did.'

'For a good reason?'

He swallowed and answered curtly, 'A very good one.'

'Harland Addington had few friends from what I have heard of him and more than enough enemies.'

'And...'

'She was in exile up on the Addington estate for years it seems and when she arrived in London last year there were many who were more than keen to court her. She made it very plain that she was not interested in finding a husband again.'

'Once bitten, twice shy?'

'The stir she created was most abhorrent to her. She did not encourage a single suitor until you.'

He laughed. 'What is it you are saying, Celeste?'

'Ask her to marry you again, Aurelian, but this time mention the word *love*.'

'How do you know I didn't last time?'

'Because if you had I think she would have accepted you.'

Chapter Eleven

Charles Mountford arrived at the Luxford town house the evening they did and he looked flustered and worried. Aurelian had sent him a note asking for a meeting.

'Thank you for coming so promptly. I appreciate it.'

'You left a mess at the tavern on the northern road, de Beaumont. Six men dead and another who could identify you when asked. Cummings is livid and wants your head.'

'My head and Violet's, it seems. But what he does not realise is we have evidence that he is a part of the plot to hide the lost French gold. He was an accomplice of Viscount Addington and I think a woman called Antoinette Herbert is still blackmailing him into doing her dirty work. I am almost certain others are involved, as well.'

'Others?'

'Cummings, for all his double-dealing, isn't the killer. Antoinette Herbert is paying somebody else to do that. I had thought at one point it might be you.'

'It wasn't.'

'I realised that when you came to warn me that Violet was in danger.'

'So they were trying to set me up, too?'

'It seems so.'

'Your *ministère* sent me a letter explaining the problem of the missing gold. If Cummings is involved, he would have seen that missive.'

'Which may be the reason this has suddenly all escalated.'

'You think he warned Antoinette Herbert?'

'I saw her at his town house last week. She left in the early morning.'

'She is his lover?'

'She was Harland Addington's lover, too.'

'Good God. I will have her house searched.'

'I don't think she would keep the gold there.'

'Where else, then?'

'She'd need someone who was used to handling such things.'

This thought rebounded into others and Lian remembered the jeweller Whitely's fear and wariness when he had registered Violet's presence in his shop. Whitely was a big man and, when Lian had shaken his hand on entering his premises, his palms had been calloused and hardened. Like a soldier. Miller had been a soldier, too. Could there be some connection there?

Whitely knew the work of George Taylor and he had been an associate of Harland Addington. It suddenly all made sense.

'Douglas Cummings has summoned me to appear

tomorrow morning before him to answer to six cases of murder. I did kill four of them but that is because they had kidnapped Violet and were trying to kill me. Eli Tucker saw to the rest.'

'Is she all right? Violet?' Mountford's question was tightly asked.

'She is now but the past days have been difficult for her, to say the least, and so she is resting upstairs.'

'Where are you meeting Cummings tomorrow?'

'At his house, which I thought unusual.'

The Minister shook his head. 'Sometimes we speak to those from a higher echelon of society in an informal environment. Given your title, there is a precedent for it.'

'If you were to be present it would be more formal.'

Mountford began to laugh. 'I can see why your *ministère* sent you here, de Beaumont, but why should I want to walk into the tiger's den for you?'

'Not for me so much as for Violet. You promised her mother that you would always watch out for her.'

'How would you know I did that?'

'Violet told me.'

Mountford sat down heavily.

'Your wife is rich and came with an unblemished pedigree. Violet's mother was the daughter of a self-made businessman and although the money was there it was not excessive. It was the hope of more that persuaded you to seek greener pastures, a decision you regretted within a month of marrying the woman who became your wife. But by then it was too late for the both of you as she had married Wilfred Bartholomew.'

'You have done your homework.'

'Now is your chance to wipe the slate clean and make amends. Violet needs to be protected and this is one way you can be certain to do it.'

'Very well.'

'Don't tell Cummings you are coming. Let us just see how it all plays out.'

After giving Mountford the details of the timing of the appointment and seeing him off, Aurelian went upstairs to find Violet. He wanted to know that she was safe with such a suddenness it took his breath away.

She was sleeping, with her hair hung in a winding braided plait against the sheet, redness magnified against the pale.

As if she knew he was there her eyes opened, awareness flooding into the green-grey depths.

'I was dreaming of you.'

He smiled at the words and crossed to the bed, sitting on the coverlet. 'Charles Mountford has just left.'

She frowned. 'What did he want?'

'I asked him to come with us tomorrow when we see Douglas Cummings. He said he would, which is a help.'

'Come to bed, Aurelian. Come and warm me up.'

Lian stripped off his clothes quickly and slid in beside her and she tipped up her head and kissed him. All the worry was pushed away and he felt himself relax. She was here and she was his. The walls he had always held around himself tumbled down until there was nothing left to hold him back.

'When I first saw you, all I could see was the light.'

He said the words softly but they were important because she had to know what he was to her before tomorrow. Taking a breath, he continued.

'I was always in darkness, you see, and it was a relief to feel the bright break through. Before you,' his voice shook but he made himself carry on, 'before you I was lost.'

Violet was astonished at his words, the quiet of night around them and one small candle burning on the table beside the bed.

She sat up.

'What is it you are saying, Aurelian?'

He came up beside her. 'I am saying that I love you and have done since the first moment I set eyes upon you when I awoke after the doctor had visited. I love your bravery and your honesty and the way you are kind. I love that you are like a warrior in your protection of family. I love you with every part of my heart, Violet, and with each breath I take.'

Tears pooled and she could feel them rolling down her cheeks. To listen to such a promise was beyond anything she had hoped for. This was not the immature love she'd felt for Harland but a real and solid and for ever love with a man who was moral and honest and good. Aurelian believed in things that were not greedy or shallow or pointless. He had fought for his truths and his life and here he was finally laying down his heart for her, giving her words that could leave no room for misconception.

'Will you marry me, Violet, and become my wife?'

'What if we don't have children?'

'Then we don't.'

It was simple and easy, the hope of it left in the hands of fate. It was as if a huge burden had been removed and she felt the weight of it slide away.

'Then, yes. I will marry you.' There was no hesitation now or uncertainty. 'I love you, too, Aurelian, and I have done since that night you made love to me when I asked for your protection. Before that I had never known what it could be like between a man and a woman.'

'Well, I have not felt it like this before, either, so perhaps it is just us.'

She laughed and leaned into him, feeling his arms coming about her and his heart beating as fast as her own.

He kissed her then, slow and deep, taking the time to let her understand what he felt wordlessly and she answered him back.

How easily he could do this, she thought smiling, this rousing her into heat. The space between her legs throbbed with desire and she closed her eyes with the ecstasy.

He would be her husband and she would be his wife. Together. For ever. Two halves of a whole. She reached down to find his centre and rolled over on top of him.

'My turn now, Aurelian,' she said, and his teeth flashed in the half-shadow.

'Mon plaisir, Lady Addington. *Fais comme tu veux.'*
My pleasure. Do as you like.

'You promise?'

'I do.'

The words were said as a vow and she smiled.

'In the church when we are married remember this moment.'

He laughed, the room fused with humour and hope.

'Love me, Aurelian.'

'I will.'

The day began badly, with the snow that had threatened falling steadily and the roads, as a result, clogged with traffic. Aurelian looked tense, and even more tense as the moments ticked on by, holding them up.

'You wish us to be early?' Violet asked this as she rearranged the shawl she wore around her neck to keep out some of the cold.

'I want to see Cummings's face when Mountford arrives, for surprise is a great revealer.'

'Of guilt?'

'And of knowledge. The Minister's presence will worry him.'

He gazed out the window and Violet saw that they were moving again and that the obstruction ahead had been cleared away. Eli Tucker and the others would be just outside Cummings's house watching and that was a relief for with Violet beside him he wanted nothing at all to go wrong.

'If there is trouble stay low and leave the room as quickly as you can. Stand next to Mountford. He is the safest of all the options apart from me, though I wish to hell that I had not let you come…'

'You couldn't keep me away and I would have followed you had you left me, for this is my battle, too.'

'Douglas Cummings will either take flight or fight when he sees Mountford. I am picking the second but I have no true knowledge of Antoinette Herbert's movements for she was not at her house at all last night.'

'You had her followed?'

'I did. Tucker is both circumspect and largely invisible even given his size.'

'But you think there are others, too, in this.'

'I am certain of it and I pray to God they are not all out in force this today.'

They had reached the house of Douglas Cummings now and alighted from the carriage, Aurelian's arm beneath her elbow as he helped her up the steps.

When they were shown into a salon to one side of the entrance he saw Mountford and Cummings standing together and his blood froze momentarily. Had he underestimated Charles Mountford's lack of morals?

Pushing Violet behind, Lian drew his pistol, levelling it at both of them, but Mountford spoke without turning a hair.

'I have explained our concerns to Douglas, Comte de Beaumont, and he is as eager to bring this farce to an end as you and I are.'

'Farce?' Aurelian could barely get the word out, his eyes skimming the further parts of the salon to qualify danger. Finding no one about to pounce upon them he lowered the gun, but still kept a tight grip upon it.

'The French gold has made fools of us all.' Cummings said this. 'Harland Addington was adamant that the bounty would be a lot more lucrative than it was but with so many involved in its disappearance there was not much room for sharing.'

'Who was involved?' While Cummings was talking it seemed a good idea to encourage him at it.

'Harland and Violet Addington for starters.' His eyes raked across Violet, hatred in the stare. 'The jewellers Miller, Taylor and Whitely and Antoinette Herbert with all her lies and deceitful plotting. Perhaps in truth she was the worst of them all.'

'She was your lover?'

Cummings laughed but the sound was rough. 'She used her body to get what she wanted and led men like bulls with hoops of gold through their noses to make certain that she held the upper hand.'

'You murdered Miller, then, while he was a prisoner?' Mountford asked, disgust in his words.

'No. I let her in to talk with him, that was all. I think it was a poison she used. There was yellow froth coming out of his mouth as he died a few hours later.'

'And George Taylor. You were seen at Chichester about the same time he was murdered?' Aurelian asked this.

Cummings blanched. 'I'd had a note to meet Whitely the jeweller there. He didn't turn up and so I left for London only to find Taylor had been murdered half a mile away from the tavern I was directed to wait at.'

'Whitely is definitely involved, then?'

'Yes.'

'But why are you? You had a job with a sense of importance in it. A family.'

'I did not imagine it would come to this. I wanted some money to pay off my bills. I've worked for fifteen years solid in this department, for God's sake, and I've never as much as had a holiday.'

'Well, you will have a long one now. I am letting you go from this day on and there will be charges laid.' Mountford sounded furious.

The door closed suddenly, with a bang that had Violet jumping as the lock turned. Aurelian crossed to wrench at the handle but no amount of movement could release the catch. Then two canisters were thrown through the window, the glass exploding into flame and smoke and sending fragments of metal through the air.

Aurelian launched himself at her and she found that she was on the floor, his body plastered across her own. With the smoke in the room Violet could not make out any other form, though she had seen Douglas Cummings fall in the first few seconds after the blast.

'Mountford?' Aurelian's voice.

'I'm here…in the…corner.'

His words sounded strange and uneven and after checking she was all right, Aurelian moved across to the Minister. With the clearing of smoke, the damage became so much more apparent, blood splattered across the room. Cummings was dead, lying face down at a strange angle to one side of the window.

Finding her wits, Violet stood, testing her legs which felt like jelly beneath her.

'Be careful of the glass shards,' Aurelian warned her and when she looked across at him his face and arms were dotted in small points of blood.

Outside she could hear people calling from the street and there was a rush of feet on the pavement. It was the fire brigade by the sounds of it and the long arm of the law would be with them.

Then the door opened and Eli Tucker held the jeweller Whitely by the scruff of his neck. 'This man threw the canisters, my lord. He was hiding in the garden.'

Alexander Whitely looked nothing like the prosperous and arrogant jeweller of a few weeks before. He was dressed in black and his face was screwed up in anger.

'She made me do it. Antoinette Herbert and her fancy promises which have all come to nothing. She even took the gold back from my shop and she promised she would not.'

'Take him outside and hold him.' This came from Aurelian as he stood sheltering Violet across the room from where Douglas Cummings lay. His arms came around her strong and solid, the smoke wafting about them making her cough.

Was there fire, too? She suddenly saw flame take on the fabric of the sofa, threatening to light the curtains.

Aurelian moved to lift the rug across the fire, jerking away the long curtains from their pelmets and stomping on them with fervour, his hands and face blackened by the task.

Finally there was a silence.

* * *

Much, much later they lay in the main chamber of the town house in Portman Square, the curtains pulled back from the window frame so that they could look outside at the night.

The glass fragments from the explosion had been removed from Aurelian's face, the process leaving him with a swollen eye and a split lip.

'So where do you think the gold will be?'

'Antoinette Herbert herself has probably stashed it away. Mountford will find it, believe me, just as he will easily track her down and he will be the one to return it to Paris.'

'What of your father?'

'That's part of the bargain I made. He will be released into Mountford's custody and he will bring him back to England.'

'To live at Compton Park?'

'No. He will want to be with my sister at the house of my aunts' outside of London.'

'My goodness. I shall inherit a family that grows by the moment, then.'

'You will like them, too, for they are good people.'

'And Amaryllis?'

'They can come home when they wish to.'

'Will the gold go to Napoleon?'

'I doubt it. Our countries might have been at war but those with true power always keep doors open for other opportunities.'

'Like you do, Aurelian?'

'Less so now than ever before. Now I know what

I want and it is only you. We can be married as soon as everyone is home again.'

She laughed at that and took his hand. 'Thank you for all you did for me today. I hope these don't hurt too much.' She touched with one finger his face in all the places the glass had punctured.

'Kiss me and they will feel better.'

When she turned to him in the semi-darkness she did a lot more than that.

Epilogue

Ten weeks later

They were married at Compton Park, under a bower of roses, in the small chapel attached to the house. Violet could not even imagine where her husband had found flowers in such abundance.

She wore pale ivory silk overlaid with the most beautiful lace she had ever seen. Aurelian told her that it made her look like an angel and that she should always be dressed in such finery.

His father had come from France, and although he was thin and pale at first, he began to look healthier with each passing day. Amaryllis and the children had also returned from being abroad, looking much better than they had in years.

Summerley Shayborne was the best man and Violet had asked Aurelian's sister to stand up with her as a bridesmaid. Berenger was sweet and young, and her laughter and enthusiasm brought joy to all the proceedings.

Celeste Shayborne arrived with vases of jasmine and camellia and fuchsia from her hothouse at Luxford, her grandmother having bound them with colourful ribbons so that the chapel looked like a fair with all the marks of celebration upon it.

Aurelian's aunts were also present, and although they seemed stern to begin with they soon lost their inhibitions and danced away with the rest of the party.

Lytton Staines, the Earl of Thornton, came to support Aurelian as did his other great friend Mr Edward Tully.

Towards midnight Aurelian led Violet out on to the glassed-in balcony overlooking a courtyard.

'I need a moment alone, my love, to give you these.'

He pulled a small green case from his pocket and when she opened the box, earrings of gold and rubies lay in the velvet baize.

'They match your hair and they were my grandmother's. Will you wear them for me?'

Her wedding ring sported a ruby, too, so they were a matching set. Smiling, she fastened the baubles to her earlobes.

'I have a gift for you, too, my love,' she whispered, the music and the scent of flowers providing a glorious setting.

This was a gift she had never thought she could have given, the perfect present on a day when they had been joined together.

She barely knew how to say the words as tears spilled down her cheeks. Happy tears. She wiped them away with one hand and took in a breath.

'We are going to have a baby,' she whispered then, as if saying the words aloud was almost sacrosanct. When she had found out she had conceived a child two weeks ago she had decided not to say anything at all to him until tonight.

Delight crossed into his golden eyes, the look on his face one that she would always remember until the very day she died.

'A baby? But you said…'

She silenced his words by laughing shakily. 'My body was barren but now it is not. With you.'

'You saw a doctor?'

'Celeste's physician. She took me to see him. I hope you don't mind that she knows? It's just I could not believe I might be pregnant and needed to make sure. He confirmed everything.'

'My God.' The words were breathless. 'A little child. Our child. When?'

'Some time in November. An almost-Christmas baby.'

'So I have been married and have learned I am to become a father on the very same day? What could ever be better than that?'

'Aurelian?'

'Yes?'

'I will love you for ever.'

'And tonight is the beginning of always.'

* * * * *

*If you enjoyed this story
be sure to check out the first book in the
Gentlemen of Honor miniseries*

A Night of Secret Surrender

*And check out these other great reads
by Sophia James*

Ruined by the Reckless Viscount
A Secret Consequence for the Viscount